Brandon moved closer to her, and Kari caught her breath. Was he going to kiss her? Maybe he thought she expected him to. He probably thought every girl he went out with wanted to be kissed. Well, he was wrong!

Abruptly, Kari moved away. "I have to go," she said. "Thanks for a nice time. See you Monday, I guess."

When the front door closed behind her, Kari leaned her head against it and sighed. She *had* wanted Brandon to kiss her. Then why hadn't she let him? Kari knew the answer very well: She was afraid she might have liked it too much.

Bantam titles in the Sweet Dreams series. Ask your bookseller for titles you have missed:

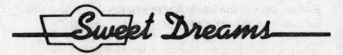

HIS AND HERS

June O'Connell

BANTAM BOOKS
NEW YORK · TORONTO · LONDON · SYDNEY · AUCKLAND

HIS AND HERS
A BANTAM BOOK 0 553 29980 8

First publication in Great Britain

PRINTING HISTORY
Bantam edition published 1994

Cover photo by Pat Hill

Bantam Books are published by Transworld Publishers Ltd., 61–63 Uxbridge Road, Ealing, London W5 5SA, in Australia by Transworld Publishers (Australia) Pty. Ltd., 15–25 Helles Avenue, Moorebank, NSW 2170, and in New Zealand by Transworld Publishers (N.Z.) Ltd., 3 William Pickering Drive, Albany, Auckland.

Printed and bound in Great Britain by Cox & Wyman Ltd., Reading, Berks.

*To my own special Kari
and to
Diane Crawford and Linda Singleton
who were in on the first sparks of this book
in New Orleans*

Chapter One

Kari Cortland hurried through the halls of Magnolia High School, dying to get out and head home. The afternoon had been a total disaster.

She ran a hand through her long curly hair and nearly bumped into Marsha Jenkins, her chemistry lab partner. Trying to forget about her problem for a moment, Kari smiled at the dark-haired girl. "Sure is warm out there today," she said.

Marsha fell in step beside her. "I just wish that southern Louisiana didn't have such hot, muggy springs."

"Sometimes I'm tempted to head for Alaska," Kari added, laughing.

As the two girls parted in the crowded hallway, Kari waved to several other kids in her class. She thought that the best part of being junior class president was meeting so many people. Usually she would linger after school and talk with classmates she knew. But today was different. She had to get out of school —and fast!

It had all started right after lunch. During fourth period, a dozen people must have asked if her mother was really dating Brandon Duncan's father. Kari scowled at the memory. If it was true, why hadn't her mom told her? How could she keep something like this from her only child?

Evidently Brandon had been griping to the entire baseball team about his dad dating her mom, and the team wasted no time spreading it around. *How embarrassing!* Kari thought dismally.

Just before she stepped out the front doors, someone tapped her on the shoulder. Kari turned to see a boy in a green letterman jacket. He grinned and raised an eyebrow. "Hey, Kari, Brandon said his dad has a date with your mom! Is that true?"

That was the last straw. *"No!"* Kari shouted. "And I'm sick and tired of hearing about it!" Then she spun around and hurried out the door. It had been like this all afternoon. If her mother had to start seeing somebody, why did it have to be an athlete's dad? Kari *hated* dumb, boring athletes, especially Brandon Duncan!

She began to run home, then slowed her pace to a jog for the last few blocks. Once she reached her house, she dashed up the stairs to her bedroom, dropping her books on the way. Flopping down on the bed, she sighed. *If it's true, why didn't Mom tell me? Why did I have to hear about it from all the kids at school?* she thought miserably.

Kari's small red dachshund, Rusty, pushed at her door until it opened, then jumped up on the bed next to her. She put an arm around him and drew him close. At that moment, she needed comfort. When Kari's father had died, she and her mother had suffered. But they had learned to be happy again, and now her mother was going to spoil everything by dating.

Kari rolled over. She'd known her mom would probably want to start dating one of these days, but why did she have to pick a classmate's father?

A short while later, Kari heard her mother come home from work. She heard her walk up the stairs and knock softly on her door. "May I come in?" her mother asked from the doorway.

Kari took a deep breath, forcing herself to remain calm. "Come on in," she said.

"Is anything wrong? I picked up your

books—they were all over the stairway. You're not sick, are you?" Mrs. Cortland asked as she entered the room and put the pile of books on Kari's desk.

"Mom, there's something I have to know," Kari blurted out. "Are you dating Brandon Duncan's dad?"

Mrs. Cortland looked puzzled, and for a moment Kari hoped that it was all a silly rumor. Then her mother pushed aside some discarded clothing and sat down in the chair next to Kari's bed. "As a matter of fact, I'm going out with him on Thursday night," she admitted.

Kari's heart sank. It *was* true. Tears began welling up in her eyes, and she willed them to stay back. "Why didn't you tell me? Everyone at school knew. Why did *I* have to be the last to find out?"

Mrs. Cortland let out a long sigh. "I'm so sorry, Kari. I was going to tell you tonight. I'm surprised that anyone else knew about it—I didn't think it was such a big thing."

"Well, it *is* a big thing. It's terrible!" Kari said angrily.

"Honey, I'm just having dinner with him—"

"I thought we were a happy family," Kari interrupted. "Why do you have to start dating?" She realized how selfish she must sound, but she was afraid that things were going to change. A date would be just the beginning. What if her mother decided to get

4

married again? "I don't want anyone to take Dad's place," she added miserably.

"Oh, Kari." Brushing her dark blond hair away from her face, Mrs. Cortland put her arms around her daughter. "No one could ever take Dad's place, you know that. And I *am* happy with you, Kari. I couldn't have survived these past four years without you. We need each other. But lately I've been thinking that it's time I started developing a social life of my own. You know, in less than two years you'll be off to college and I'll be here alone."

A wave of guilt washed over Kari. "Oh, Mom, I'm sorry," she said. How could she be so thoughtless of her mother's feelings? Still, she hated the idea of her mom dating Brandon's dad. "I didn't mean you shouldn't have friends. But couldn't you go out with somebody else?"

"What's wrong with Chad—er, Mr. Duncan?" Mrs. Cortland asked.

Kari winced at the sound of his first name. "Well, to begin with, his son goes to my school and he's a real jerk."

Mrs. Cortland looked surprised. "Really? I heard Brandon was somewhat of a star in every sport."

"He's just a dumb jock, but a lot of the girls act like he's some kind of Greek god," Kari said, frowning.

5

"Just give him a chance. Maybe if you got to know him . . ."

"I don't *want* to know him. He's so stuck on himself that he doesn't even talk to anyone except his dorky jock friends."

Mrs. Cortland sighed.

"What about Mr. Sloan down at the cleaners? He doesn't have a wife, and he's good-looking," Kari suggested.

Laughing, her mother shook her head. "Now don't turn into a matchmaker on me! I can handle my own social life."

Not if all you can dig up is Brandon Duncan's dad, Kari thought.

"Regardless of what his son is like," Mrs. Cortland continued, "Mr. Duncan is very nice—and after all, we're just going to have dinner."

"How did you meet him anyway?"

"He's a client my company does business with." Mrs. Cortland stood up and started for the door. "Now I'm going to make us an early dinner. I have a meeting tonight." Pausing in the doorway, she added, "Kari, this isn't going to spoil things for us, I promise."

"Don't bother making dinner for me," Kari said. "I'm going to eat at Wendy's. We've got two impossible math problems to finish before tomorrow's trig class."

"All right. But don't stay too late. It's a school night, remember."

When her mother had left the room, Kari hopped off the bed. She felt a little better, but not much. She'd probably feel a lot better after she shared this catastrophe with Wendy Sawyer, her best friend.

Picking up a spray bottle, Kari misted her mop of curly, sun-streaked hair, trying to coax it into a new style without success. With a sigh, she put the bottle away, snatched her books, and hurried downstairs.

At Wendy's house, Mrs. Sawyer opened the door and pointed Kari in the direction of the loud music. Taking the stairs two at a time, Kari burst into her friend's room. Wendy was sitting on the bed, reading a copy of *Seventeen*.

"Argh!" Wendy screeched, and the magazine flew out of her hand. "You scared me out of an inch of growth!"

Kari laughed. "We can't let that happen, or you'll shrink away to nothing."

Wendy was only five feet tall, a good six inches shorter than Kari. Her big brown eyes and dark hair, cut in a short, dramatic style, gave her the striking looks of a model. Wendy desperately wanted to work in the fashion industry and as Kari looked at her friend, she was sure she'd make it someday.

"Did you figure out the trig problems?" Wendy asked.

Kari shook her head. "I decided we'd better

attack them together. But first I have to tell you about the disaster at home."

Wendy's eyes widened. "What happened?"

"You mean, you haven't heard? I thought the whole school knew!"

"I haven't heard a thing," Wendy said. "What is it?"

"It's terrible, that's what! My mom is going out with Brandon Duncan's dad."

"You've got to be kidding!" Wendy exclaimed. "Is he as cute as Brandon?"

"Come on, Wendy! Brandon may be nice looking, but you know what those jocks are like. Anybody whose friends call him *Bubba* can't be very bright. And he's so stuck up."

Wendy wrinkled her nose. "That nickname *is* kind of stupid. But maybe Brandon isn't."

Kari groaned. "Now you're sounding like my mother."

Wendy gave her a mischievous look. "I just don't understand how Brandon can be so good in every single sport. Don't you think it might be interesting to date the Bo Jackson of Magnolia High?"

"Come on, Wendy! I wouldn't date Brandon Duncan if he begged me. Besides, I don't even know him."

"Is he in any of your classes?"

Kari nodded. "Yeah, we have chemistry together. But he sits in the back of the room with the other sports goons, and he never answers any questions or anything."

"Just because you had that one incident with that football player last year doesn't mean all athletes are creeps," Wendy pointed out.

"That one *incident* got me into a lot of trouble," Kari said angrily. "The teacher thought that since my lab partner cheated on a test, I had, too. I've never been so humiliated in my life."

"But you straightened it out with Mr. Jarven. And anyway, nobody really thought that you cheated."

"Maybe. But that's the last athlete I'm ever going to have as a partner for *anything*," Kari vowed.

"In any case, it wouldn't hurt to be friendly," Wendy said.

"Why would I want to be friendly? It's *his* father who might ruin my life!"

Wendy shrugged. "Okay. Have it your way." Grinning, she added, "I'd go after Brandon myself if I didn't have my eye on Mike Prentice in Student Council. In the meantime, guess we'd better hit the books."

"Yeah. Between the two of us, we ought to be able to figure out this assignment," Kari said, thinking that if math problems were the only thing she had to worry about, she'd be okay. But trigonometry was a cinch compared to the problem she faced at home.

After a short break for dinner, Kari and Wendy finished their trigonometry homework. Kari enjoyed working with Wendy—they could actually study together and get something done. The time had passed quickly, and glancing at her watch, Kari saw that it was half past nine.

"I have to go," she told Wendy. "I promised Mom I wouldn't be late."

Wendy yawned. "I guess that's enough studying for me, too. Just remember what I said about Brandon. Try to be nice."

"I'll think about it," Kari said as she gathered up her belongings.

"That sounds like 'No I won't' to me."

Kari frowned. "Sorry, but I can't see myself getting all friendly with him."

"At least say hi," Wendy urged. "Who knows? Maybe he'll get his buddies to quit making cracks about your mom and his dad."

"I guess I could speak to him. Anything to get those guys off my case," Kari said. "I'm not sure I could stand another day like today."

When she arrived home, a light was burning in the front hall, but Mrs. Cortland was still at her meeting. The house seemed lonely. *When Mom starts dating, there might be a lot of nights like this*, Kari thought. She didn't like that idea at all.

In the kitchen, Kari poured herself a glass of milk and got out a box of graham crackers. Taking them to the table, she shared the crackers with Rusty while she thought about her mother wanting a social life of her own. Kari could understand that. But if her mom was going to go out with someone, it had to be the right person, not Brandon Duncan's dad.

Well, Kari decided, *I guess it's up to me to find a man for Mom.*

Chapter Two

The next day as she stood in the hallway not far from the science room, Kari saw Brandon sauntering down the hall with two of his friends. Grudgingly, she had to admit that most girls would die for his dark, curly hair and those long, thick eyelashes. She bit her lip. If she was going to make a move, she had to do it now.

Pacing herself, Kari reached the door at the same time as Brandon. "Hi," she said, looking up at him and smiling.

Brandon glanced at her, and the animated expression on his face faded. He said nothing. With a curt nod, he stepped past her into the room.

Staring after him, Kari fumed. Who did he

think he was, anyway? All she had done was try to be friendly, and he'd treated her like dirt. What a jerk!

Gritting her teeth, Kari walked to her seat, trying to act as if nothing was wrong. She carefully set her books on her desk, though she wanted to throw them straight at Brandon.

"Hey, what's with you?" Marsha Jenkins, Kari's lab partner, asked. "You look like you were just bitten by a rattlesnake."

"Something like that," Kari muttered. She figured Brandon was probably in the back of the room, laughing at her with his stupid friends. Deliberately dropping her pencil, Kari turned in her seat so she could see Brandon when she picked it up.

Instead of snickering with his friends, Brandon was looking right at her. Surprised, she met his gaze for a few seconds before he scowled and turned away. "Oh, he makes me so mad!" Kari said aloud as she grabbed the pencil and turned back to face the front of the room.

"Who's got you so steamed up?" Marsha asked.

"Brandon Duncan! Do you know anything about him?"

Marsha glanced toward the back of the room. "Not much more than you. Just that he's gorgeous, he's Magnolia High's star first baseman, and he plays on just about every other team. One of the girls in my English class says he's sort of quiet."

"Quiet? I can't believe that!" Kari said. "He's always talking to his dopey friends."

Marsha shrugged. "I never thought much about him. Since I met Jeff I haven't been looking."

"Well, I'm not looking, either! I can't stand stuck-up athletes!" Kari snapped.

Just then Mr. Adams, the chemistry teacher, came into the room. Kari opened her notebook, but she couldn't concentrate on a word he was saying. Instead, she kept fuming about Brandon and his dad. Finally she managed to calm down by telling herself that she didn't have anything to worry about. Maybe her mother's date with Mr. Duncan would be a disaster.

On Thursday night, Kari peered out her bedroom window, waiting for Mr. Duncan to arrive. She hadn't tried to talk her mother into canceling her date, but she certainly wasn't going to put her seal of approval on it by meeting him at the door.

Rusty trotted over to join her, and Kari tickled his ears while she stared out the window. At last a dark green car turned onto her street and drove slowly toward her house. "Oh, no, a Mercedes!" Kari groaned. "Why couldn't he drive a beat-up Chevy or something?"

Moving back so she couldn't be seen, Kari watched as Mr. Duncan got out of the car and walked up to the porch. She had to admit that Brandon's dad was good-looking. He had the same dark, curly hair as Brandon, flecked with gray. He was also muscular like Brandon—his broad shoulders seemed to more than fill his sport jacket. *Why couldn't he have been scrawny and ugly?* Kari thought.

The doorbell rang, and Rusty bounded out of the room, barking his usual protest.

"Kari!" Mrs. Cortland called on her way downstairs to answer the door. "I'd like you to meet Mr. Duncan."

That was the last thing Kari wanted to hear. She dashed into the bathroom and turned the shower on full force. If she was in the shower, then she couldn't possibly meet anybody. "Can't come right now, Mom," she hollered.

A few minutes later, when she thought the coast would be clear, Kari came out of hiding and hurried to the window again. As she watched Mr. Duncan open the car door for her mother, Kari grimaced. She had to admit her mom looked great, especially as she gave Mr. Duncan a brilliant smile. Kari had been hoping this date wouldn't go well, but already it looked like it was starting off *too* well.

*   *   *

Later that night, Kari finished her chemistry assignment and tried to work on her English composition. But she couldn't help wondering what restaurant Mr. Duncan had chosen, and if they had gone anywhere afterward.

Around ten o'clock, Kari put on the tea-kettle so the water would be boiling when her mom got home. They could sit down over a cup of tea and Kari could hear about how awful—she hoped—her mother's date was. Fifteen minutes later Kari heard the front door open, and Mrs. Cortland called a cheery "Hello." Casually Kari walked into the hall. "Want a cup of tea, Mom? The water's hot."

"Sounds good!" Her mother followed Kari into the kitchen.

Kari prepared two mugs of tea, and she and her mother sat down at the table. "That was a pretty fancy car," she said.

Mrs. Cortland smiled. "Mmmm. Nice, wasn't it?"

Kari frowned. Her mom was definitely not acting like her usual sensible self. "Sort of expensive. Is he rich?" Kari held her breath, hoping Mr. Duncan didn't have one more thing to add to his list of good points.

"It's a company car. And it's none of our business if he's rich or not," her mother said.

"Did he—uh—did he try anything?" Kari asked.

Mrs. Cortland burst out laughing. "Oh,

Kari! What a question! You'd think you were the mother and I was the daughter. No, he didn't try anything. He was a perfect gentleman."

Kari stared at her mother. She looked positively starry-eyed, like a teenager after a big dance, and Kari realized that it was the first time she'd seen her mom so happy in ages. "I'm sorry, Mom." She leaned over and kissed her cheek. "I'm glad you had fun."

Later as she lay in bed, Kari remembered that starry-eyed look. She didn't want to ruin her mother's happiness, but she was sure she could find someone her mom would like just as much as Mr. Duncan. *There must be a lot of unattached men around,* Kari thought. *I'll have to start looking first thing tomorrow.*

The next morning Kari met Wendy at the corner to walk to school.

"How did the big date go?" Wendy asked immediately.

Kari sighed. "She liked him."

Wendy squealed, but when she saw Kari's grim expression, she tried to be serious. "What did you do while they were out?"

Kari wrinkled her nose. "I spent the whole night doing homework."

"Why didn't you come and stay with me?"

"Well, I wanted to see what Mr. Duncan was like—"

"Hey! Were you spying on them?" Wendy interrupted.

"I was not spying! I was just checking him out, that's all. Anyway, do you know any single men?"

Wendy laughed. "The school's full of them!"

"No, I mean *older* men, around Mr. Duncan's age."

"Oh, I get it," Wendy said. "You mean like for your mother?"

Kari nodded. "I figure if I can find her someone else, maybe Brandon's dad will just fade out of the picture."

Wendy grinned. "Sounds like an excellent plan. I'll keep my eyes peeled for somebody cool—and *old!*"

Kari couldn't keep her mind on her classes that morning. She was too busy trying to make a list of suitable men for her mother. She looked thoughtfully at Mr. Ellis, who was lecturing on the Spanish-American War. She'd put him on the list if he was about twenty years younger. Kari grinned for a moment, picturing her mom with the gray-haired, stoop-shouldered history teacher.

But by the time Kari walked into the student government office for third period, she hadn't come up with a single name. Wendy joined her a few minutes later and asked, "Any ideas yet?"

18

Kari shook her head. "No, but I'm sure I'll think of someone soon. What about you?"

"Not so far, but I'm working on it. Listen— are you going to the game this afternoon?" she asked. "It's a big one, and there's a pep rally at noon."

"I couldn't care less about baseball—or baseball *players*," Kari said. "But I guess it doesn't look good for the junior class president not to show, so I guess I'll be there."

Wendy grinned. "Good! Too bad it's not basketball season. I love to see all the guys in those cute little shorts."

Kari gave her a mock scowl. "Wendy! You're supposed to be thinking about school spirit, not guys!"

Wendy grinned. "So we each have our priorities. Come on—let's go paint."

Making banners for the Magnolia High Gators games was a Student Council responsibility, and Kari was helping Wendy's publicity committee. As she picked up a set of wide markers, Kari said, "I think I'll make one that says, 'Brandon Duncan is a jerk!'"

"You wouldn't!" Wendy said.

Laughing, Kari admitted, "No, I wouldn't, but I'd like to!"

The girls gathered up their supplies and headed outside to the open quad, where the rest of the committee members were waiting. "Let's get this done so we can go to the pep rally," Wendy said.

19

For the next hour the publicity committee worked at a frantic pace to get all the banners done. When the bell rang, Kari, Wendy, and the others headed for the gym where the pep rally was to be held. The cheerleaders ran through their cheers and dance routines. When the Magnolia High Gators trotted onto the floor, the crowd of students cheered and whistled.

"Guess we don't have to worry about school spirit," Wendy yelled to Kari over the din.

The team took seats on the platform by the band. One by one they were introduced by the head cheerleader, who gave a glowing tribute to each player as he came forward. Brandon Duncan was last. When he stepped to the microphone, the crowd went wild.

Kari looked at Wendy and made a face. "Looks like I'm definitely in the minority here."

"Better believe it!" Wendy said, laughing.

The noise died down as the student body waited to hear what Brandon had to say about the game that afternoon. It wasn't much. "Southfield's going to get whipped," he stated. "They don't stand a chance against the Gators!"

"That was so dumb," Kari whispered. "Let's get out of here. This is making me sick!"

"Can five hundred fans be wrong?" Wendy asked innocently.

"They're just crazy about him because he's

a hotshot athlete," Kari said. "If he was just a plain student, he wouldn't be so popular."

Wendy giggled. "A guy who looks like that could hardly be called a 'plain' student!"

Kari knew that her friend was right. Even without Brandon's star status, the girls would still be crazy about him because he was so handsome. But Kari would take someone who was smart any day, and she certainly didn't have to worry about that person being Brandon Duncan.

Chapter Three

The following Thursday, Kari came home from school after a Student Council meeting. Turning her key in the lock, she opened the door and called, "Mom! I'm home and I'm starved!"

When there was no answer, she dumped her books in the hall and headed for the kitchen.

On the table, Kari spied a note propped up on the basket of silk tulips that served as a spring centerpiece. As she read the words, her heart fell.

Kari:
Catching an early movie with Mr.
Duncan. Won't be late. Dinner in the
oven.

Love,
Mom

"Again?" Kari said aloud as she wadded up
the note and tossed it in the trash can. Why
couldn't Brandon's dad leave her mother
alone?

Taking the meat loaf and vegetables out of
the oven, Kari set it on the table and found
the salad her mom had left in the refrigerator. She served herself, then began shoving
the food around on her plate. Somehow she
wasn't very hungry anymore. It was no fun
eating alone.

She felt Rusty nuzzling her ankle, begging
for attention. Absentmindedly, she scratched
his head, thinking about what her mother
had said last week: "I'm just having dinner
with him on Thursday night." *Yeah, right,*
Kari thought. *And a second dinner on Saturday night, and several phone calls over the
weekend.* Mr. Duncan was monopolizing all
of her mom's free time. But Kari had to
admit that her mother had seemed awfully
happy lately. Several times she'd heard her
singing—something her mother hadn't done

since Kari's father died. Dating did seem to lift her mom's spirits.

And any man would take up a lot of time. But she'd feel a whole lot better about it if the man wasn't Brandon Duncan's dad.

"Come on, Rusty," she called to the dachshund who pranced at her heels. "You'll just have to help me think harder to find some other eligible men. I have to replace Mr. Duncan as soon as possible, before Mom starts getting serious about him."

The next afternoon Kari came straight home from school alone. She didn't have a Student Council meeting, and Wendy had gone to her modeling class. As Kari came in the door, her mother called down from her bedroom. Surprised, Kari went upstairs. "Mom! What are you doing home so early? You're not sick, are you?"

She found her mother sitting on the bed surrounded by department-store bags. "No, I'm just fine," she said. "I had to pick up some papers in Overton, and it was too late to go back to the office, so I decided to do some shopping."

"I noticed. What did you do, buy out the store?" Kari asked with a smile.

Laughing, Mrs. Cortland opened a bag and pulled out a soft jersey dress in a muted raspberry color. "What do you think?"

"I love it! It's so different than those suits you always wear to the office."

"How about the color? Is it too much?"

"It's perfect for you. Hold it up!"

Mrs. Cortland stood up and held the dress against herself. "I haven't bought anything like this since . . ." her voice trailed off.

"Since Dad died," Kari finished for her. "I know. It's about time you had something pretty."

She watched the glow return to her mother's face. The raspberry color was very becoming to her, and Kari liked the softness of the style. "What else did you get?"

"Maybe I overdid it, but I haven't shopped in such a long time, and I just couldn't decide which to put back," Mrs. Cortland confessed. She spread out two pairs of slacks, a frilly top, and another dress. Then she reached for the last bag. "This might have been a splurge, but I couldn't resist it."

Kari gasped at the floral dress her mother took out of the bag. She couldn't picture her wearing such a youthful style.

"Well, I guess it isn't right for me," Mrs. Cortland said, seeing her daughter's expression.

"Oh, no," Kari said quickly. "It's lovely, Mom. I was just surprised because it's so . . ."

"Young. I know." Her mom sighed as she folded the dress and started to put it back in the bag. "But it made me feel so good when I tried it on."

"Then you should keep it," Kari told her, taking the dress from her. "You'll look terrific in it when you go out somewhere fancy—" She stopped. Of course, that's why her mom had bought all these new clothes! She'd bought them to wear when she went out with Mr. Duncan. Kari forced a smile. "I'll just hang it up for you."

"Thanks, honey." Mrs. Cortland hugged Kari. "I'll hang up the rest. Then I'll start dinner."

On her way out of the bedroom, Kari felt confused. She was happy for her mom, but she felt sad, too. Things were definitely changing in their lives, and there didn't seem to be anything Kari could do about it.

Rusty streaked past her down the stairs, barking. When he jumped up on the front door, she knew it was time for the mail. Since he was just a puppy, the dog had been barking at the mailman. In spite of scoldings, Rusty apparently felt it was his duty to guard the house.

Opening the door, Kari saw the mailman stuffing several letters into the box. "Hi, Sam. Anything for me?" she asked.

"Wait till that beast quiets down." He reached into his pocket, pulled out a dog biscuit, and tossed it to Rusty, who snatched it and scampered back inside. "You still looking for a letter from Prince Charming?" Sam joked.

"I'd be happy with a letter from anyone." Suddenly, Kari took a closer look at Sam. He was kind of attractive, in a mailman sort of way. And he was taller than her mom. . . . "Sam," she asked hesitantly, "are you married?"

He stared at her. "Me? Married? Not for the last ten years."

"What happened to your wife?" Kari blurted out, and then blushed as she realized how nosy she sounded.

Sam didn't seem to mind. "She took off with this rich guy. Just because we get the mail through, doesn't mean we're rewarded for it." He grinned and handed Kari several letters and magazines. "See you."

"Yes—see you soon." Kari closed the door and stepped over Rusty who was busily gnawing on his biscuit. Now how could she get her mother to notice that Sam the mailman was just as eligible as Mr. Duncan?

When the phone rang late Saturday afternoon, Kari raced into the kitchen, but her mother picked it up first. From the expression on her mother's face, it was obvious to Kari who was on the other end. She groaned and slowly left the room, but she couldn't help hearing her mother's end of the conversation.

"It's really not a very good day," Mrs. Cortland was saying. After a long pause, she said, "Well, I suppose I could ask her."

Kari frowned. Somehow she knew she wasn't going to like whatever her mom was going to ask.

"Kari," Mrs. Cortland called. "I need to talk to you."

Trying to keep her expression blank, Kari came in from the hall and sat down at the kitchen table. Her mother sat in the chair opposite her. "This is a lot to ask, honey, but would you mind terribly if I went on a picnic tomorrow with Mr. Duncan?"

"But tomorrow is Sunday!" Kari cried. "Sundays belong to the two of us!" Kari and her mother always spent Sundays together. They usually planned something special, but the important thing was that they were together. Now her mom wanted to break their tradition and go out with Mr. Duncan again. Kari felt crushed.

"It's his company picnic and . . . and he wants me to meet the people from his office," Mrs. Cortland said. "But if it really bothers you, I'll tell him I can't go," she added quickly.

Kari sighed. "No—go ahead. I'll find something to do. But I hope it's just this once."

Kari saw her mom's face light up, and Kari realized again how happy her mom seemed lately. Shaking her head, she got up and started out of the kitchen.

"Kari," Mrs. Cortland called after her.

"There's something else. When the mail came this afternoon, I talked to Sam, and he told me you were asking if he was single. You're not matchmaking, are you?"

"I was just curious," Kari said casually. "He's not bad-looking and he's about your age."

Mrs. Cortland rolled her eyes. "Kari! I am *not* interested in Sam. Just because I'm going out with Mr. Duncan doesn't mean I'm ready to play the field. One man is enough for now."

"That's what I'm afraid of," Kari muttered to herself.

On Sunday afternoon, Kari wandered aimlessly around the house. It seemed so empty without her mom. She'd tried to do her homework but couldn't seem to concentrate. Finally she called Wendy. When her friend answered, Kari asked her if she was busy.

"Just watching an old movie on TV. Aren't you doing something with . . . Oh, I forgot. This is picnic day."

Kari scowled. "Yeah. You want to go to the mall or anything?"

"Sure. I've seen this dumb movie four times," Wendy said. "I'll get the car. Ten minutes, okay?"

"I'll be outside." Kari hung up and hurried to change. Then she grabbed her purse and ran downstairs to wait for Wendy.

Wendy pulled up in front of the house a moment later.

"I just had to get out of here," Kari explained as she jumped in.

"I understand. It must seem weird to have your mom go off with *him* on your special day."

"She said it's just for this one Sunday, but I'm not so sure," Kari said glumly.

Wendy nodded. "You never can tell. Hey, aren't you going to ask me about my interview at the modeling agency?"

"Oh, I forgot all about that. How did it go?"

Wendy wrinkled her nose. "Good and bad. Of course, they mentioned my height—I already know I'm too short. But they *did* say they'd see about getting me a job."

"That sounds good." Kari tried to sound encouraging. She knew how much Wendy wanted a modeling assignment.

When they reached the mall, the girls first headed for an accessory shop because Wendy needed a belt for her new denim jumpsuit.

Kari browsed the pierced earring racks while Wendy tried on every belt in the store. Finally making up her mind, Wendy paid for her purchase, and they wandered down to a boutique that specialized in clothing for teenagers.

Holding up a sweater with flowers embroidered around the neck, Kari said, "I wish my allowance would stretch so I could afford this."

"I think I saw one like it at the outlet on Martin Road," Wendy said as she looked through the rows of pants. "Maybe we can go there later."

"Let's go upstairs to the pet store now," Kari suggested.

Wendy grinned. "You'll have to keep me from buying something. If I come home with one more animal, my mom's threatened to put me out on the street!"

Kari laughed. Wendy had two dogs, three cats, and an assortment of small caged animals at home. She just couldn't resist anything soft and fluffy.

On the escalator, Kari glanced up and caught her breath. Hanging over the railing on the second floor was a group of guys from Magnolia High, and one of them was Brandon Duncan. He was talking to his friend Jake, who was also on the baseball team. As Kari watched, she saw Jake poke him and nod in her direction.

"There's Brandon," she muttered to Wendy.

Wendy looked up. "He's certainly checking you out."

Kari lifted her chin defiantly and returned Brandon's stare. She couldn't read any expression on his face. Suddenly, he nudged Jake, and they and the other guys walked away.

In the pet store Kari thought about Brandon. What had he been thinking? He hadn't looked angry. In fact, he'd almost looked right through her. Then she shook her head impatiently. She wouldn't waste her time wondering about *him.*

"Hey, you want to go down to the yogurt shop before we leave?" she asked Wendy.

"Yum!" Wendy said. "I feel a sudden urge for a large chocolate with crushed Snickers on top."

Kari grabbed Wendy's arm and started to walk fast. "You're making me hungry. Let's go!"

Once they were settled at a table with their yogurts, Kari said, "It's strange. Since my mom started dating Mr. Duncan, I seem to bump into Brandon everywhere. I never saw him around before."

"Well, you know, his dad left him alone today, too," Wendy said.

"I didn't think of that." Kari wondered if Sunday was a special day for Brandon and his dad the way it was for her and her mom. Maybe Brandon was upset, too.

"You know, Kari, I was just wondering . . ." Wendy licked her spoon and leaned over. "You don't think your mom and Mr. Duncan would do anything stupid—like get married?"

It took a few seconds for Wendy's words to sink in. "Married!" Kari exclaimed.

"Well, it could happen," Wendy said. "Then

32

you and Brandon would be stepbrother and sister."

"Stop it, Wendy!" Kari wailed. "That's impossible. *Please* tell me it is!"

"I shouldn't have mentioned it," Wendy said quickly. "It was just a thought. You know me—I'm always shooting my mouth off."

"My mom would never do that to me." But even as Kari spoke, she had a sick feeling and her stomach knotted. Could her mother possibly marry Mr. Duncan?

Chapter Four

When Kari got home, she sat in the kitchen, thinking about what Wendy had said. She just couldn't let her mother marry Mr. Duncan, and she needed help. As much as Kari hated to ask Brandon for anything, she decided to call him right away, before she lost her nerve.

She looked up Chad Duncan in the phone book, and slowly, reluctantly, dialed the number. Brandon answered, and Kari was surprised at how pleasant his voice sounded.

"Hi, Brandon. This is Kari Cortland," she said. Trying to keep it light, she went on, "What's going on with our parents?"

"Well, it sure wasn't *my* idea," Brandon snapped. He didn't sound pleasant anymore.

Taken aback by his abruptness, Kari swallowed, then continued. "I guess neither of us is happy about it."

There was a long silence, and Kari wondered if Brandon was going to hang up on her. Finally he said, "My dad doesn't need some woman trying to get her hooks into him."

"What?" Kari shrieked. "My mom is *not* like that! It's your dad who's chasing *her*!"

"Yeah, right. Dad and I were getting along fine, just the two of us, until *she* came along."

"Wrong!" Kari insisted. "*He's* been monopolizing all my mom's time!"

"My dad's not spending a lot of time here, either. He's always with *her*!"

Kari took a deep breath, trying to calm herself down. As evenly as she could, she said, "Well, at least we agree on something. So what are we going to do about it?"

After another long silence, Brandon mumbled, "I don't know."

"Why don't we meet tomorrow after school and see what we can come up with?" Kari suggested.

"I have baseball practice every day after school," he said.

"I can wait," Kari said promptly. "I have a lot of stuff to do in the student government office."

"Yeah, that's right. You're junior class president."

"Do you have a problem with that?" she asked defensively.

"No. In fact, it's pretty cool."

Thrown off by his compliment, Kari almost forgot that he hadn't answered her question. She decided to act as if he'd agreed. "I'll meet you at the Pizza Palace tomorrow right after practice, okay?"

After a pause, Brandon said, "I'll be there."

As she hung up the phone, Kari thought about his attitude. Although Brandon was obviously just as upset as she was about their parents, she certainly didn't like the things he'd said. Imagine him thinking her mother was doing the chasing! Brandon should be glad his dad was dating such a wonderful person!

Eager to tell Wendy about her upcoming meeting with Brandon, Kari hurried to her friend's house on Monday morning so they could walk to school together. As they started off, Kari shared her news.

Wendy raised her eyebrows. "Ooh, sounds exciting."

Kari gave her a playful punch on the arm. "Cut it out! This is business."

"You never know," Wendy said with a grin. "Maybe—just *maybe*, you'll find you like him."

Kari gave her a dirty look. "Me like a jock? Never!"

"Speaking of jocks, my family's going camping in three weeks. Mom said I could invite you."

"That sounds great," Kari said. "Give me all the details."

As they walked along, Wendy chattered about the camping trip, but Kari's mind kept wandering. "Have you found any men yet that would be good for my mom?" she asked finally.

Wendy shook her head. "Nope. All the good-looking older guys are already married."

"Well, keep your eyes open." Then Kari told Wendy about Sam the mailman.

"Okay, scratch Sam. But don't give up hope. We'll find someone else," Wendy assured her.

Kari finished her work in the student government office a little early, so she headed for the baseball field. Careful to stay out of Brandon's—and Jake's—sight, she watched the last part of practice. The Gators were playing an intersquad game, and she noticed the good-natured banter among the guys. They looked as if they were having fun.

When the team headed for the gym, Kari hurried across the street to the Pizza Palace. She bought herself a soda and found a table in the back corner. Fifteen minutes later, Brandon walked in. His hair was still wet from the shower, and Kari couldn't help noticing how handsome he was. He spotted her and nodded, then got a soda and spoke to several kids at a table near the front before he ambled back to where Kari was sitting.

"Well, I'm here," he said ungraciously.

"Thanks for coming," Kari said with a friendly smile. She figured if they began by arguing, nothing would be accomplished.

He pulled out a chair and sat down. "I don't think there's anything we can do."

"We can at least talk about it."

Brandon scowled. "What good is talk?"

Losing her patience, Kari slapped her hand on the table. "Look, Brandon, if we don't at least try to do something, we could end up stepbrother and sister!"

Brandon looked shocked. "I—I never thought of that."

"Well, think about it now," Kari snapped.

"Married. Jeez." Brandon shook his head. "You're right—we have to do something. I've thought about trying to break them up, but I don't have any idea where to start. I've already told my dad I don't like her," he said gloomily.

Kari glared at him. "How could you not like my mom? You don't even *know* her! She's everything a man could want."

Brandon glared back. "*Some* man, maybe, but not my dad! We don't need any woman in our lives. Women just foul everything up."

38

"Well, a man would foul up *our* lives, too," Kari announced. "So let's decide what we can do. I've thought of a couple of things."

"I figured you'd have it all worked out," Brandon said with a sneer.

Kari's temper flared. "What's that supposed to mean?"

He shrugged. "You're obviously the organized type."

"Well, at least I've been *trying* to come up with some plans!"

"Okay, okay. Let's hear them." Brandon propped his chin on his hands, staring at her grimly.

"First," Kari said, "I thought we could try to answer the phone all the time and if one of them calls, tell them the other one isn't home."

"Forget it. They'll just keep trying. Besides, they can call each other at their offices."

Kari frowned. "Well, it was just an idea. Then I thought when your dad calls, I could pretend to mistake him for someone else. That way he'd think there were a lot of other men in her life."

Brandon just laughed. "You don't know much about men, do you?"

Kari fidgeted under his gaze. "What do you mean? What's wrong with my idea?"

"If Dad thinks a lot of guys are after your mom, it will probably make him jealous and then he'd call even more."

Kari hadn't thought about that, but she had to admit he might be right.

"I don't know—I guess it wouldn't hurt to try it. What other neat things have you planned?" Brandon asked.

"Well," Kari said, "you might try to find some other woman for your dad."

"Why would I want to do that? I just told you I don't want *any* woman messing up our lives!"

"I thought that's how I felt, too. But now I've decided Mom needs somebody to have fun with—but *not* your father."

"Are you trying to tell me my dad isn't good enough for your mom?" Brandon yelled, then glanced over his shoulder, checking to see who might have heard. Lowering his voice, he added, "My dad is really cool."

"I'll take your word for it," Kari said. "But he's just not right for my mom."

"If you want to find someone else for your mom, okay. But I want my dad to stay single."

Exasperated, Kari said. "I'm *so* glad I have your permission!"

Out of the corner of her eye, Kari saw Brandon's buddy Jake come in the door and peer around. When he saw them, he started shouting, "Hey, Bubba! I been looking all over for you." He eyed Kari curiously.

Brandon stood up. "I'm finished here, right, Kari?" When she nodded, he turned to Jake.

"Hey, man. Want to go take a look at your carburetor problem?"

Watching them walk away, Kari sighed. Some help Brandon had been! She wondered if he would do anything at all. He was upset about their parents' relationship, but would he follow through? Kari felt that she couldn't depend on him. She'd just have to step up her own efforts to find another man for her mom—and try to intercept any calls from Mr. Duncan.

When Kari walked in the door of her house, the phone was ringing. Dropping her books, she ran to answer it. On the other end a deep voice said, "Hello, this is Jack Thompson, down at the hardware store. I just wanted to tell you that your lawn mower is all ready to go."

Kari hadn't known their lawn mower was broken. But Mr. Thompson certainly had a nice voice. Maybe he was a possibility. "Did my mom bring it in? You know—*Elizabeth Cortland?* She's a blond, attractive *widow*."

"Yes, I remember your mom very well," Mr. Thompson said. "She dropped it off last week to have it sharpened. Tell her she can pick it up anytime."

"Thanks, Mr. Thompson, I will," Kari said, then hung up.

What a great voice! she thought. *So rich and deep. If only I knew what he looked like....*

41

Suddenly an idea popped into Kari's head. She dashed out the door and ran over to Wendy's.

"Wendy, I need you! You've got to come with me," she said as she burst into her friend's bedroom.

Wendy was listening to her portable CD player. Pulling off her headset, she asked, "Hey, what's up?"

Kari slumped into a chair and tried to catch her breath. "I want you to go with me to check out Mr. Thompson. We have to find out what he looks like!"

"Hold it! Who's Mr. Thompson?" Wendy started digging her sneakers out from under her bed.

"Male Possibility Number Two!" Kari said. "He has a dreamy voice—he called about the lawn mower. We have to go down to the hardware store and check him out."

Wendy finished tying her laces. "Okay. Sounds interesting."

The two girls quickly walked to the neighborhood shopping center. Kari stopped outside the store next door to Handy Hardware. "Let's just casually walk by and take a look, then maybe we'll go in. Try to act natural."

"Spying on somebody is *not* a natural thing to do," Wendy said.

"We're not exactly spying. We're just finding out what he looks like." Kari started walking again. "Pretend we're having a conversation."

Wendy giggled. "We *are* having a conversation!"

As the girls sauntered past the hardware store, Kari murmured to Wendy, "I'm not really cut out for this kind of thing."

"Maybe we should have worn dark glasses and trench coats," Wendy said, laughing. "What are we going to do now? There were three men in there."

Kari nodded. "Yeah." She paused. "Wendy, we have to go in."

Wendy gave her a look. "Right. What are we going to do? Just walk in and say we're not interested in buying anything—we're just checking to see if Mr. Thompson is good-looking?"

"Let me think." Kari thought for a moment. "Okay, let's go. I have a plan."

"Oh, no!" Wendy rolled her eyes. "Not another one!"

Grabbing Wendy's arm, Kari pulled her toward the door. "Come on. I'll do the talking."

They walked into the store and stepped up to the counter. "May I please speak to Mr. Thompson?" Kari asked in a businesslike manner.

A stocky man with short blond hair came forward. "That's me. What can I do for you, young lady?"

"I'm Kari Cortland, *Elizabeth Cortland's* daughter," she said. "You called to say our lawn mower was ready. My friend and I came to pick it up."

"Right, I just spoke to you. I'll get it." He went into a back room while Kari watched. He seemed nice, and he was sort of cute. Too bad he wasn't taller.

Wendy poked Kari in the ribs. "Not bad," she mouthed.

Giving Wendy a don't-say-anything look, Kari started digging in her purse.

Mr. Thompson returned with the lawn mower and began to write out a slip. Suddenly Kari gasped. "Oh, no! I'm so embarrassed—I seem to have left my wallet at home."

"No problem," Mr. Thompson said. "Take the mower and pay me later. I know you live in the neighborhood."

"You do? Er . . . I mean, it wouldn't be right to do that. I'll have my mother pick it up one day soon on her way home from work."

Mr. Thompson laughed. "Anything to get out of cutting the grass, right?"

"Oh, you're on to me," Kari said with a sheepish grin. "My mom will get it. Her name is *Elizabeth Cortland.*"

"I got it," Mr. Thompson said as he pushed the mower into the back room again. "Enjoy your afternoon," he called over his shoulder.

As soon as they were outside the door, Kari and Wendy collapsed onto a bench in front of a clothing store. Laughing so hard she could hardly talk, Wendy gasped, "That was an Academy Award performance, Kari! You should try out for the school play."

"My plan worked," Kari said triumphantly. "His looks don't match his voice, but he's cute enough. Do you think my mom might like him?"

Wendy shrugged. "Maybe. Who knows? But what if he's married?"

"He wasn't wearing a ring—I checked his left hand." Kari frowned. "Now all I have to do is figure out how to get Mr. Thompson to ask Mom for a date."

Chapter Five

When the phone rang the next night, Kari answered it and heard Mr. Duncan asking for her mother. "Oh, hello, Mr. Thompson," she said brightly. "Mom's at a meeting tonight." She was glad that her mom was really out.

"Er . . ." Mr. Duncan hesitated. "This is Mr. *Duncan*, not Mr. Thompson. Will you please tell her I called?"

"I'll leave her a note," Kari said in her sweetest voice.

As soon as she hung up, she scribbled the message and then dropped the note into a drawer in the table. For a moment she cringed at doing something so sneaky, but then she decided it was okay to be sneaky for a good cause.

Mrs. Cortland got home late, and Kari made sure she was in bed so her mother wouldn't ask her if anyone had called. She smiled. Mr. Duncan sure had seemed surprised when she'd mentioned Mr. Thompson's name. She couldn't wait to tell Brandon what she'd done.

The next day, she met him in front of her English classroom. For once he wasn't with Jake. "Any new developments?" he asked.

Surprised that Brandon had actually been the first to speak, Kari told him about his father's phone call last night. "But we're going to have to come up with a lot more than that," she added.

"Yeah. My dad has two tickets to some play on his dresser. He's probably planning to ask your mom. He's bound to get hold of her sooner or later."

"If we can just slow things down a little, it will help," Kari said. "At least until I can find her someone else."

Brandon frowned. "What's wrong with my dad? Why do you want to get rid of him so badly?"

"Well, I . . ." Kari couldn't tell Brandon it was because she didn't want her mother dating the father of a dumb, stuck-up athlete. Actually, Brandon wasn't acting that stuck-up now, and she was beginning to think he wasn't all that dumb.

"Never mind," he said before she could

47

come up with a suitable response. "I don't want her in my dad's life, either. We manage just fine all by ourselves."

Kari stuck out her hand. "Fine. Then we're partners."

Brandon looked at her hand a moment before he shook it. "Just keep making more plans," he said, then walked away down the hall.

Kari stared at her hand. She was glad Brandon had sealed the bargain, but she hadn't been prepared for the tingle she'd felt when he took her hand. "No way," she muttered as she entered the classroom. She wasn't getting all gaga over some jock, especially not Brandon Duncan.

Mr. Burns, the English teacher, distracted Kari's thoughts from Brandon when he assigned a composition to be written in class. Usually, English was one of Kari's easiest subjects, but today she had trouble concentrating. The assignment, to review a movie, was interesting, however, and finally Kari was absorbed in writing about the movie she'd seen with Wendy last week.

As she handed in her theme, Kari suddenly had an inspiration. Movies! Why not invite her mom to the movies on a night when she thought Mr. Duncan might ask her out? If she kept her mother very busy, she wouldn't have time for Brandon's dad.

That night Kari asked her mom to go to

the movies with her on Friday night. Mrs. Cortland was both pleased and surprised. "That sounds nice. But don't you usually do the movie thing with Wendy?"

"Well, yeah, but I thought maybe you and I could do something—just the two of us." Kari certainly didn't want her mom including Mr. Duncan. "We haven't done anything together for a long time."

"Well . . . I was going to a concert with Chad." Mrs. Cortland hesitated. "But I'm sure he will understand if I explain how important it is to you."

"That's great, Mom!" Kari threw her arms around her mother and gave her a big hug. It had worked! She'd actually put a stop to a date with Mr. Duncan. Now she had to think of more things to do.

"By the way," Mrs. Cortland said. "When I picked up the lawn mower this afternoon, I had a chat with Mr. Thompson. He didn't think you knew that he and I have been friends for a long time."

"You have?" Kari said, startled.

Her mother went to the closet to take out the vacuum. "Yes—he's married to a woman I work with."

"He's *married*?" Kari's heart sank. "I didn't see a ring."

Mrs. Cortland frowned. "Kari, you're not doing it again, are you? Matchmaking, I mean."

"Who, me?" Kari said innocently. "What-ever gave you that idea?"

As she started up the stairs to her room, she muttered under her breath, "I can't *believe* he's married!" So much for Possibility Number Two. But somewhere there had to be a single man her mom would like.

During the next two weeks, Kari spent every available minute with her mother. She dragged her to the mall on shopping sprees and talked her into taking long walks and bike rides in the park. Kari even treated her mom to dinner at a local restaurant—anything to keep her away from Mr. Duncan. And she made regular reports to Brandon, who seemed to be doing a pretty good job of keeping his father busy, too.

By the end of those two weeks, both Mrs. Cortland and Kari were exhausted. Kari was falling behind in her homework, and she felt guilty when Wendy complained that they never saw each other anymore. And in spite of everything, her plan wasn't a complete success.

As they were having breakfast one morn-ing, Mrs. Cortland told Kari that she planned to go to a play with Mr. Duncan that night.

Drat! Kari thought. "But we were having such a good time together," she said.

"We've had a wonderful time," Mrs. Cort-land said with a smile. "But we're not Siamese twins, you know. You need to be with your friends, and I need some time with mine, too."

"But, Mom . . ."

"We'll still do things," her mother assured her. "Just not every night."

When her mother had left for work, Kari grabbed her books and raced to Wendy's house. She found her friend in the kitchen finishing her breakfast.

"You're early," Wendy said as she drank her orange juice.

"I know. Can we leave now? I need to talk to Brandon before school."

Raising one eyebrow, Wendy gave Kari a knowing look. "You've been doing an awful lot of talking to Brandon lately."

"You know what it's about."

Wendy nodded. "But the rest of the kids at school don't. Everyone's buzzing about the two of you. They think you've got something going."

Kari's mouth dropped open. Could the kids really be pairing them up as a couple? "Why didn't you tell me?"

"I tried to several times," Wendy said as she gathered up her books. "But I haven't seen much of you since you decided on all this togetherness with your mom."

Kari sighed. "I'm sorry. But I can't imagine people thinking that Brandon and I . . ."

"Well, they are."

They left the house and started walking to school. "I haven't even told you my news! The modeling agency called—they have a job for me!" Wendy said.

"That's great!" Kari cried. "Why didn't you tell me before?"

"Like I said, I've hardly seen you lately."

Kari silently promised herself she'd do better, and they talked about Wendy's future modeling career most of the way to school.

Then they began discussing Kari's determination to find Mrs. Cortland a different man to date. "I've just about run out of ideas," Kari confessed. "I didn't know it would be so hard to find someone who's the right age, single, and not ugly."

"I keep checking out every man I meet." Wendy's eyes sparkled. "The young ones for me and the older ones for her!"

Kari shook her head. "No wonder Mom didn't start dating sooner. There just isn't that much choice out there. What am I going to do, Wendy? I just can't let her end up marrying Mr. Duncan. I've accepted the fact that she's going to date him, but I don't want it to go any further."

"What does Brandon say about it?" Wendy asked.

"He's as much against it as I am, but he doesn't have many ideas. Just like a jock!"

"Kari, you can't go on blaming all athletes because of one bad experience," Wendy said.

"Oh, yes I can! That stupid football player just lounged around and watched me do all our biology experiments. And I wrote all the reports, too."

Wendy sighed. "I know, I know, he was a jerk."

"Jerk, jock—it's the same thing."

"Not necessarily," Wendy said. "I don't think Brandon's a jerk."

Kari smiled weakly. "At least I'm talking to him."

"I think it could turn into *more* than talk if you'd just let it. Half the girls in the junior class would trade places with you in a minute."

Kari scowled. "I will never, ever date an athlete."

"Your loss," Wendy said cheerfully.

When they reached the school, Kari said, "I'm going to find Brandon. See you at lunch." As she walked quickly down the corridor she saw Brandon ahead, taking some books out of his locker and talking to Jake. *Why does Jake always have to be hanging around?* she thought.

Jake winked when he saw her and leaned against the locker. "Here's your girlfriend, Bubba."

Brandon glared at his friend. "I'll see you in class," he said.

With a grin, Jake ambled off down the hall, and Brandon turned to Kari. "What's up?"

"I've been keeping my mom busy, but I can't do it anymore," Kari said. "She wants more space."

He shrugged. "It was nice while it lasted. Dad's actually been home at night. We've even eaten dinner together for a change."

Kari smiled. "So have Mom and I. I hate eating by myself."

"Me, too," Brandon said. "Maybe we should have gotten together. I mean, so we didn't have to eat alone," he added quickly.

"I guess we're lucky they haven't suggested we all go out to dinner together like one big happy family."

Brandon grimaced. "My dad's already mentioned that. He just hasn't said anything to your mom yet."

Just then the bell rang, and Brandon slammed his locker shut. "Where's your homeroom?"

"Over in *B* wing."

"Come on, let's get going. I'm heading that way, too."

Kari noticed several students eyeing them as they walked to the other side of the building. She was sure the kids were speculating on how her "romance" with Brandon was going. *Some romance,* she thought.

"Well, see you," Brandon said as he left

her at her homeroom. "Keep me posted and I'll let you know if anything develops on this end."

Kari watched him walk away. Brandon seemed to be enjoying their consultations, and she had to admit that she was, too.

When Kari arrived home after school, Rusty did not meet her at the door the way he usually did. Surprised, since he always greeted her as if he hadn't seen her in weeks, she went to find him.

Hearing a whimper from the kitchen, Kari wasted no time getting to him. When the little dog saw her, he gave a pathetic cry as he struggled to get up and walk.

"Rusty, baby, what's wrong?" she asked, scooping him up in her arms. When she stroked his head, Rusty yelped in pain. Kari lifted one ear and inspected it carefully, finding nothing. But when she touched the other one, he yelped even louder. "Uh-oh. It looks like you've got one of those awful foxtail burrs in your ear again."

Rusty nestled into the crook of Kari's arm as she gently stroked his back. She carried him into the den and put him on the couch while she called the vet.

After making a six o'clock appointment, she cradled Rusty in her lap while she waited for her mom to come home from work. Kari hoped her mother wouldn't be late—she knew the little dog was in great pain.

Forty-five minutes later, Kari heard Mrs. Cortland's car pull into the drive. She scooped up Rusty and met her at the door. "Rusty's got a foxtail in his ear again," she said. "I think it must be infected. He has a fit every time I try to touch it."

"Poor little guy!" Mrs. Cortland set down her briefcase and scratched Rusty under the chin. "Did you call Dr. Evans?"

"Yes—he's expecting us at six," Kari said. "Can we go now? Maybe he'll take Rusty a little early."

"Of course," Mrs. Cortland said, and they hurried to the car.

When they got to the animal clinic, they didn't have to wait very long before Dr. Evans's nurse took them to a treatment room. The vet immediately began to examine Rusty.

"You're right," he said after peering into the dog's ear. "Those foxtails can work right into the eardrum."

As he spoke, Kari looked into the vet's deep brown eyes. She had been so concerned about Rusty that it had taken a few minutes for her to focus on Dr. Evans. Why hadn't she thought of him before? He was the right age, and she knew he wasn't married. And best of all, he was even better looking than Mr. Duncan!

When Dr. Evans went back to checking

Rusty, Kari nudged her mother and mouthed the words, "He is *so* cute!"

Mrs. Cortland rolled her eyes, but then she nodded and they both had to stifle their giggles.

As Dr. Evans glanced up and grinned at them, Kari wondered why she hadn't noticed his dynamite smile before. She hoped her mom had noticed it, too. As Possibility Number Three, Dr. Evans was definitely the most eligible man Kari had found yet. Now if only her mom was interested. And if she was, could Kari get the two of them together?

Chapter Six

"Oh no, it's seven-thirty!" Kari jumped out of bed the next morning and flung on her clothes. After a restless night worrying about Rusty, she'd overslept. Gulping down a breakfast shake, she glanced at the clock and moaned. Why did she have to be late today of all days? There might not be time to see Brandon and tell him about Dr. Evans.

Wendy had gotten a late start, too, so the two girls almost ran all the way to school. "For someone who isn't interested in Brandon, you're sure in a rush to see him this morning," Wendy pointed out.

"That's only because I have something really important . . ." Kari began. But by this time Wendy was halfway down the hall, so Kari headed the opposite way.

She was amazed to find Brandon standing by her locker.

"I—I'm really late this morning," she stammered, thinking how dorky she must sound. He'd have to be *really* stupid not to realize that.

"No kidding," Brandon said. He looked very glum. "I've been waiting for about fifteen minutes."

"You have? Is there any news?"

"Yeah. My dad's taking your mom to dinner at La Cherie next Saturday night," he told her. "I heard him making the reservations."

"Oh, no!" Kari moaned. "That's the most romantic spot in town!" The French restaurant overlooked the river and had a boardwalk along the water. They definitely didn't want their parents to go there. "Why did he make the reservation so far ahead of time?"

Brandon shook his head. "Beats me. Maybe they fill up fast."

"Will the moon be full then?" Kari asked anxiously.

"The moon?" Brandon stared at her. "What's the moon got to do with it?"

"Everything. A full moon would be much too romantic," Kari stated. "We've got to stop them."

"Well, for starters, I've already canceled

the reservation," Brandon said with a flicker of a smile.

Kari was really surprised. He was finally going into action! "That's great. But what do we do next?"

Brandon's smile disappeared. "You got me. Any ideas?"

Kari thought hard. "I don't like doing this, but I think I'll have to leave my mom a phony message saying your dad called and canceled."

"Hey, that might work!" Brandon said. "I just hope she doesn't call him to ask him why."

"Me, too," Kari said. "Oops—there's the bell. We'd better get moving."

"Okay. See you at lunch."

As Brandon headed for his homeroom, Kari stared after him. *What did he mean, he'll see me at lunch?* she wondered. They usually didn't talk so often. But come to think of it, she hadn't had a chance to fill him in about Dr. Evans. Lunch would be as good a time as any.

When Kari went into the cafeteria at noon, she saw Brandon leaning on one of the posts near her usual table. She decided to talk to him before she got her lunch—and before Wendy arrived.

"Hi," he said, smiling. "How's it going?"

Kari put her books on the table. "Well, I had a quiz in math, and we're real busy in student government, getting ready for elections."

There was an awkward pause. Then Brandon said, "Say, I was thinking . . ."

"You have another idea?"

"Not exactly. I just—I mean, we never get to talk very long between classes, and I'm in kind of a hurry now . . ."

"Do you want to meet after school again?" Kari asked.

Brandon shook his head. "I was wondering if we could maybe take in a movie Friday night."

Kari could hardly believe her ears. A movie? Did he mean a date? No, of course not. It wouldn't be a real date—it would be a *planning* date. There was no reason why she shouldn't go just this once. Then she remembered Wendy. Since Kari had been with her mother the last two Friday nights, she'd promised to go bowling with her friend.

"Sorry—I can't," she said. "I already have plans. Besides, I make it a policy never to go out with athletes."

Brandon looked surprised. "Why not?"

"I'd rather not talk about it, if you don't mind," Kari said. She certainly wasn't going to explain anything to him, but she *did* want to tell him about Dr. Evans. "What about Saturday afternoon?" she suggested. "If you want to—if you're free, that is."

Brandon studied the pole he'd been leaning against and rubbed his thumb over a name someone had scratched there. "Uh-uh. I have something I have to do every Saturday afternoon."

"Do you have a job?" she asked.

"Not exactly. It's just something I do," he said. Apparently he didn't want to explain anything to her, either.

Shrugging, Kari said, "Okay."

Brandon took a deep breath. "What about a Saturday night movie?"

Without thinking she said, "That's great!" and then wondered why she was so enthusiastic. "I mean, I guess that will be all right."

"I'll pick you up about seven-thirty," Brandon said, then walked away to join Jake and several other guys at a table in the corner of the cafeteria.

Kari jumped when Wendy poked her in the ribs. "Hey, Earth to Kari! Come in, please."

Kari turned to her friend. "You'll never guess what just happened!"

"I bet it had something to do with Brandon," Wendy said, grinning. "Tell me about it while we get our lunch."

"He asked me to go to the movies," Kari said as they headed for the salad bar.

"And of course you turned him down."

Stealing a glance at Brandon, Kari shook her head. "No. I said I'd go. We're going to do some more planning."

Wendy raised an eyebrow. "At the *movies*?"

Kari felt herself blushing. "We'll probably go somewhere afterward and talk."

"Yeah, right." Wendy gave her friend a knowing look. "Just don't make plans for next weekend, okay? Remember, we're going camping."

"I haven't forgotten." Now Kari was having second thoughts. Why had she said she'd go to the movies with Brandon? It would just make it look as if the gossip about them was true. And it wasn't true at all. They were nothing more than partners in a plot to break up their parents.

When Kari got home late that afternoon after finishing up some student government business, her mother wasn't there. Kari knew she had to do something about the dinner at La Cherie. Not wanting to lie to her mother in person, she scribbled a note saying that Mr. Duncan had called, canceling their dinner date for next Saturday night.

Mrs. Cortland had gone straight from work to pick up Rusty from the veterinary clinic. Kari was hoping that something might develop between her mother and the handsome vet. Maybe they would become better acquainted—maybe Dr. Evans would even ask her mom for a date. Mrs. Cortland might even accept—she'd seemed to like him a lot yesterday.

Hearing the car in the driveway at last, Kari bolted out the front door and raced over. Rusty had already jumped up and pressed his nose to the window. When he saw Kari, his tail wagged so hard, he looked like a windup toy.

"Rusty!" she cried, opening the car door and scooping the dog off the front seat. "You're all better!"

Mrs. Cortland got out. "Dr. Evans said they had to put him out to remove the burr. But as soon as he woke up, he was fine." She handed Kari a small package. "You'll have to be in charge of his medicine."

"Did Dr. Evans look as gorgeous as he did yesterday?" she asked as they walked to the house.

Mrs. Cortland smiled. "He *is* a good-looking man, isn't he?"

When she didn't say anything else, Kari demanded, "Well?"

"Well, what?" Grinning, her mom added, "Were you hoping we'd have a steamy rendezvous in the back room?"

"*Mom!* You know I wasn't!" Kari glanced at her mother. "But I did think that maybe he'd ask you out."

Mrs. Cortland sighed as they went inside. "Kari, you can't choose a man for me. I have to do that myself."

"I was just pointing out a few possibilities."

Her mother sat down on the sofa. "Honey, why don't you like Mr. Duncan?"

"It's not that I don't like him," Kari said, choosing her words very carefully. "I just don't think he's right for you."

Mrs. Cortland shook her head sadly. "I was hoping you'd change your mind. You know, it's hard to date someone when your daughter—in my case, my whole family—is against him."

A wave of guilt washed over Kari. She didn't want to make her mom unhappy. If only she could be seeing someone other than Brandon's dad! At least her mother was concerned about how Kari felt. A tiny flicker of hope rekindled itself. But what if she couldn't find anyone to replace Mr. Duncan?

Later that evening, Mrs. Cortland came into the kitchen where Kari was doing her homework at the table. She looked puzzled. "Kari, I don't understand this message from Chad—Mr. Duncan."

Now Kari *really* felt guilty. She tried to smile. "I guess something came up," she mumbled.

Her mother shook her head. "The strange part is . . . I don't remember him asking me to dinner."

Kari froze, thinking, *I can't believe this! I*

canceled the invitation before Mr. Duncan did the inviting!

"Hmmm. Well, maybe I just forgot." Still shaking her head, Mrs. Cortland read the note again as she walked out of the room.

Kari panicked. What should she do now? Mr. Duncan was sure to call and invite her mother to dinner, and when he did, she'd know Kari was interfering with her life. Even worse, she'd know Kari had lied.

Then she thought, *What if Mom calls him now?* She had to get to the phone first! Racing to her room, Kari held her breath as she picked up the receiver. Hearing the dial tone, she heaved a sigh of relief and immediately called Wendy. As soon as her friend answered, Kari explained that they needed to talk for a long time until it was too late for her mom to phone Mr. Duncan.

"I was just going to call you anyway," Wendy said. "Something *awful* happened this afternoon. I just can't *believe* they'd do this to me!"

"Who? What'd they do?"

"Oh, Kari, I'm so embarrassed. I felt like such a fool! You know that job the agency got for me? They said I was to be a product spokesperson. Well, it turned out when I got there that it wasn't for a modeling job." She paused. "It was to pass out free samples at the grocery store!"

"That's terrible! But something else will

come along," Kari assured her. "Did anyone from school see you?"

"No, thank goodness," Wendy said. "That would have been *totally* humiliating."

They talked for about an hour. When Kari hung up, she glanced at the clock. It was ten-thirty, and she figured that it was safe now.

So far, so good, she thought. But when Mr. Duncan *did* invite her mother to that dinner, she was sure there would be fireworks.

Chapter Seven

After school on Friday, Kari joined the crowd of kids heading for the baseball diamond and climbed to the top of the bleachers. She and Wendy were going to watch the game, and Kari wanted to find an out-of-the-way seat where Brandon wouldn't spot them. She didn't want him to get the silly idea that she'd come to see *him.*

Minutes later, Wendy bounced up the steps, waving and calling to all her friends. Kari sighed. There might as well have been a large arrow pointing directly at them. She looked down on the field where Brandon and Jake were playing catch. Maybe he wouldn't notice her at all.

"Hi!" Wendy said as she sat down. "Are we

here to support the whole team, or just one particular player?"

Kari scowled and punched her friend's arm. "We're showing school spirit, the way we did at the last game."

Wendy giggled. "I believe you. Sure I do!"

"Shhh! Don't talk so loud." Kari took a quick glance around. "I don't want anybody to hear you. Let's just watch the game, okay?"

The Oakdale High Rockets came up to bat first, and the Gators held them to one hit. When it was the Gators' turn, Kari found herself waiting eagerly for Brandon to step up to the plate. She knew how good he was, but since she deliberately hadn't been to a home game in weeks, she wondered how he'd been hitting lately.

Wendy grabbed her arm. "Look! Brandon's up now."

"So I see," Kari said, trying to sound nonchalant. But she couldn't ignore the excitement building inside her. Why was she feeling this way? She tried to convince herself that there was nothing special about Brandon. Then why was her pulse racing as if she'd just run around all the bases?

Brandon took his place in the batter's box. Even from her seat high above third base, Kari could see the muscles in his arms ripple as he gripped the bat.

Brandon swung at the first pitch—and missed. Wendy clenched her fists. "Rats! He's trying too hard."

Two pitches later, Brandon had one ball and two strikes against him. "Come on, Brandon!" somebody yelled. "Let's do it! Hit a home run."

But on the next pitch, Brandon struck out. A collective groan rose from the Gators fans.

Kari turned to Wendy. "I guess he's not such a hotshot after all," she said, concealing her disappointment.

"Everybody's entitled to an off day every now and then," Wendy told her. "Brandon usually hits more homers than anyone else. I don't know what's wrong with him today."

In the third inning when Brandon came up to bat, he knocked the ball over the left-field fence. As he trotted around the bases to the wild cheers of the crowd, Kari jumped up and down and yelled along with Wendy and the rest of the Gators fans.

"He really *is* good!" Kari admitted when they sat down.

When the game was over, the Magnolia Gators had won by a score of five to one. Brandon had contributed four hits and two more runs. Kari clapped with the others as the team ran off the field. Brandon was a big hero, all right, but he didn't seem to be like the other athletes she'd known. Could he really be different?

As soon as she got home, Kari opened a book and sat down in the kitchen, waiting for the phone to ring. She was tired of guarding the phone all the time, but she couldn't let Mr. Duncan invite her mom to the dinner he'd supposedly canceled.

An hour later, the phone rang, but it was just Wendy. "I have some great news!" she said. "It's about my future in modeling. Believe it or not, somebody wants to use me!"

"That's fantastic!" Kari cried. "You got an actual modeling assignment?"

Wendy hesitated. "Well, not exactly. But it's a step in the right direction."

"Come on, tell me what it is."

"A woman from the agency called right after I got home. They have another assignment for me."

"Are you sure it's not more free samples? I heard the supermarket was looking for a short brunette," Kari teased.

"Just wait until I'm on the cover of some hot magazine," Wendy grumbled.

Kari faked a sob. "You'll be too busy signing autographs to be my friend."

"Be serious. This time it's for a photo shoot tomorrow. They want me to come to the Crescent City Studio."

"In New Orleans?" Kari asked, impressed.

"No, they have a branch here in town."

"What are you going to be doing?"

Wendy giggled nervously. "I don't know exactly. But I'll be paid for it. And it will be great in my portfolio."

"I hope it's something good," Kari said. "Maybe we *will* get to see you in a magazine. But while you're still my friend, don't forget that we're going bowling tonight," she added. "See you around eight."

At six o'clock, Kari gave up her vigil by the phone. It would be just her luck if Mr. Duncan called tonight while she was out with Wendy. Or else he'd call when her mom was in the same room and she'd have no choice but to hand over the phone.

Kari put her book away and started to heat up the leftovers from last night. A few minutes later, her mother walked in.

"Is it ever muggy out there!" Mrs. Cortland said as she took off her jacket and unfastened the top buttons of her blouse.

Kari took a pitcher of lemonade out of the refrigerator and poured a glass for her mother. "Here, Mom. This should cool you off."

Taking a long drink, Mrs. Cortland sighed. "That tastes wonderful. Thanks, honey. Let me go get into something comfortable and I'll be back to help with dinner."

A few minutes later she came into the kitchen again, wearing a colorful sundress that Kari had never seen before. "Do you like it?" her mother asked. "I know I shouldn't have bought anything else, but it was in Sherman's window and I fell in love with it."

"It's very nice," Kari said. Then she had an awful thought. "Uh—are you going out with Mr. Duncan tonight?"

Her mother shook her head. "No social life for me this weekend. Chad left on a business trip yesterday." She reached in the drawer for an apron. "He won't be back until Sunday night."

Kari sat down abruptly at the table. While she'd been guarding the phone, Mr. Duncan was out of town! Why hadn't Brandon told her that his dad was away? Excusing herself, she raced upstairs to call him in private. When he answered, she noticed again how nice his voice sounded.

"Hi, Brandon. It's Kari," she said. "Hey, how come you never mentioned your dad was out of town? I've been sitting here for hours, ready to pounce on the phone in case he called."

Brandon groaned. "Oh, wow! I'm sorry. With the game and all, I forgot to say anything about it."

"That's okay. It didn't kill me," Kari said. "By the way, I've been thinking—maybe I should meet you at the movie tomorrow instead of you picking me up here. I don't want my mom to know we're going out together."

"Why not?" Brandon said, sounding a little annoyed.

"Because if she thinks we're going out on a date—even though it isn't *really* a date—she might think it means I approve of her going out with your dad," Kari explained.

After a pause, Brandon said, "I guess you're right."

"So I'll meet you in front of the theater tomorrow night at seven-thirty."

"Okay. See you there," Brandon said. Right before he hung up, he added, "Oh, and Kari?"

"Yes?"

"Thanks for coming to the game this afternoon."

Saturday evening after dinner, Kari stood in the middle of her room, trying to decide what to wear for her "planning session" with Brandon. She kept telling herself that it didn't really matter, but she didn't want to look like a nerd.

She heard the front door bang open and Wendy bounding up the steps with Rusty barking at her heels. Moaning loudly, she flopped onto the bed on top of a pile of discarded clothes.

"What happened?" Kari asked in astonishment. "You didn't miss the photo shoot, did you?"

"Oh, I got there on time, all right." Wendy pulled a pillow over her face and mumbled something Kari couldn't hear.

Kari lifted the pillow. "Don't be so dramatic. I can't understand a word you're saying!"

"You'd be upset, too," Wendy wailed. "Here I thought I was going to get some pictures for my portfolio, but they didn't want to photograph *me*. All they wanted was someone to help with a session of *baby photos*!"

Kari stared at her. "You took baby photos?"

"No!" Wendy moaned again. "It was my job to get them to laugh. I spent the whole afternoon shaking rattles and making funny faces for a bunch of *babies*!"

Kari tried to stifle her laughter, but keeping a straight face was impossible. She couldn't help it—she broke up.

"Go ahead, laugh." Wendy glared at her, sitting cross-legged in the middle of the clothes. But soon the corners of her mouth turned up in a wry smile. "At least I got paid for it."

"Well then, those modeling lessons aren't a total loss. Now give me some advice." Kari reached into the pile and pulled out a red top and a black miniskirt. "What do you think? Too dressy?"

Wendy cocked her head to one side. "Yeah. What about your new jeans?" She began to paw through the heap of clothes.

Together they finally decided on the jeans and a flowered top, with a sweater in case the theater was too cold.

Fifteen minutes later, Kari was dressed.

"You look great," Wendy said as she got off the bed. "If you're ready, we can go get the car and I'll drop you off at the theater."

The girls walked to Wendy's house, and Wendy borrowed the car. As they drove to the theater, Kari twisted her hands, and wondered again if going to the movies with Brandon was a good idea. Half a block from their destination, she said, "Just let me off here. I'll walk the rest of the way."

Wendy pulled over to the curb. "Don't want him to see me, huh? Remember, if he doesn't offer to bring you home, I'll be right by the phone. And if he *does* take you home, be sure to call me first thing tomorrow morning and tell me everything."

"As soon as I wake up," Kari promised.

After Wendy drove off, Kari waited outside the theater, trying not to look as nervous as she felt. Checking her watch, she saw that it was getting close to movie time. Where was Brandon, anyway? Walking over to the glass-framed posters, she pretended to study the coming attractions. She wondered if he'd been having second thoughts about this whole thing, too.

Kari winced when she saw several kids she knew. Waving and smiling at them as they bought tickets and went inside, she wondered if they thought it strange to find her hanging around the theater all by herself. It didn't matter—when they saw her with Brandon, it would be all over school on Monday. *If* they saw her with Brandon.

Glancing at her watch again, Kari debated whether to buy one ticket and see the show alone, or call Wendy and ask to be picked up. She could hang out at Wendy's for a while, then go home.

Suddenly she heard someone calling her name. Whirling around, Kari saw Brandon running across the parking lot. "Sorry I'm late," he said between breaths. "Before he left, my dad made up this huge list of things for me to do, and some of them had to be done today."

Kari laughed. "I thought you were going to stand me up."

"I wouldn't do that to you." He turned toward the box office. "Let's get our tickets, okay?" He stepped up to the ticket window. "Two, please."

So he's taking me out, Kari thought. Maybe this *was* a date after all.

"Want some popcorn?" he asked as they stepped into the lobby.

Kari nodded. She loved popcorn at the movies.

When they entered the theater, the previews were in progress, so they found seats halfway down. "This okay?" Brandon whispered as he led the way to center seats. Kari sat next to him and put her sweater across her lap.

Brandon balanced the large tub of popcorn on the arm of the seat, steadying it with his hand. Kari could feel his arm touching hers, and a tingle ran through her. She shook her head. This wouldn't do at all!

When the main feature started, Kari was glad they'd decided on a comedy. She certainly didn't want to see a lot of romantic stuff sitting next to Brandon. The plot of the movie involved a funny mix-up of several couples in a Mediterranean country. Soon both Kari and Brandon were laughing, and Kari no longer felt self-conscious. But she *was* starting to feel cold. Why did they always have to keep movie theaters so freezing? She shivered a little.

Brandon whispered, "Are you cold?" He trailed his finger along her arm. "You've got goose bumps."

Kari shivered again, but not because she was chilly.

Brandon leaned closer. "Do you need help with your sweater?" he asked.

His hair brushed her cheek, and Kari's pulse raced. She nodded, hoping he didn't know the effect he was having on her.

Brandon took her bulky pullover sweater and tried to help. But as he pulled it over her head, Kari realized he'd gotten it off center. Her head was stuck in an armhole! With one arm already in a sleeve, and Brandon tugging on the sweater, Kari felt like she was in a straitjacket. The more they struggled, the worse it got. Giggling, she gasped, "I'm stuck! Help me take it off!"

"What? I can't understand you." Brandon kept pulling, and Kari giggled even harder.

"Will you two settle down?" someone whispered from behind them.

Kari finally struggled out of the sweater by herself and started all over. Without Brandon's help this time, she got her arms in the sleeves and quickly popped her head out of the neck opening. The stricken look on Brandon's face sent Kari into another wave of laughter, and she clapped her hand over her mouth to keep it back. Brandon began to laugh, too.

"*Quiet!*" the voice behind them hissed angrily.

They swallowed their giggles, and Kari willed herself not to look at Brandon for fear she'd burst out laughing again.

For the next hour, Kari spent more time watching Brandon's hand than the screen.

First, he moved it to his half of the armrest. Then he inched it over closer to where her own hand lay just below his on her knee. Was he going to hold her hand? If he did, what would she do? Did she really want to hold hands with Brandon? To her own amazement, Kari decided that she did. But Brandon didn't touch her at all, and she was oddly disappointed.

They walked out of the theater after the movie was over. "It was really good," Kari said, but she had to admit that she hadn't paid much attention to the film.

"Yeah, great," Brandon agreed. "Listen, we need to talk. Want to get a soda and some pizza?"

"I'd love to," Kari said, then wondered if she sounded too eager.

"Did you drive?"

"No—my friend Wendy dropped me off."

"Then we'll take my car," Brandon said. "It's at the back of the lot." He pointed off to the left, and they started making their way through the parked cars. "You like pepperoni on your pizza?"

"Actually, I prefer mushrooms," Kari admitted.

Brandon grimaced. "We'll order it by the slice, then."

When they reached his car, Brandon fished in his jeans pocket for the keys. Frowning, he dug in another pocket, and then another, mumbling, "Where the heck . . . ?"

Kari happened to glance through the car window. "Uh—Brandon," she said softly, "I think we have a problem."

There, in the ignition, were the keys.

Chapter Eight

Brandon slapped his hand on the hood and leaned against the fender. "I can't believe I did that!"

"It's no big deal," Kari said.

He forced a smile. "I'm really sorry, Kari. You're taking this pretty well."

"You don't have an extra key in one of those magnetic boxes that goes underneath?"

"No," Brandon said with a sigh. "My dad told me I should do that, but I never got around to it."

"So what do we do now?"

He peered into the window again. "If Dad wasn't out of town, I could call him to bring the other set of keys."

Kari shrugged. "If he were here, he'd

probably be out with my mom tonight anyway."

"You're probably right. Hey—I have an idea," Brandon said. "I'll call Jake. If he's home, he can pick us up and take us to my house so I can get the spare keys."

"Or I could call Wendy," Kari suggested.

"No, that's okay. I don't want to bother her, but I don't mind bothering Jake."

Just what I need—Jake with his smart remarks, Kari thought, annoyed.

Using the pay phone on the corner, Brandon dialed his friend's number. Kari hoped Jake wouldn't be home, but when Brandon started talking, she knew they were going to have the pleasure of Jake's company whether she liked it or not.

Brandon hung up and turned to Kari. "He'll be here soon." He grinned. "I'll never hear the end of this one!"

They walked back and waited by the car. True to his word, Jake arrived in less than ten minutes. Vaulting out of his old convertible, he took one look at Kari and then poked Brandon in the ribs. "Hey, Bubba! You didn't mention you had company."

Brandon looked uncomfortable. "That's because I was concerned about the car. You know Kari Cortland, right?"

"Yeah," he said with a sly grin. "I know Ms. Junior Class President. Who doesn't?"

Kari wanted to dig a hole and drop out of

sight. Why couldn't they have called Wendy? At least she wouldn't have made any cracks.

They all piled into the front seat of Jake's convertible and drove back to Brandon's place. While the boys went inside, Kari took the opportunity to look at the house. It was a big, brick ranch with a wide lawn and lots of shrubs and trees. Suddenly a sick feeling washed over Kari. She realized that if her mother ended up marrying Mr. Duncan, he'd probably want them to live here instead of in the Cortlands' much smaller home. *Oh, no!* she thought. *I never want to leave the house I grew up in!*

Kari forced herself to calm down. Moving here could only happen *if* they got married, and she and Brandon weren't going to let that happen.

Brandon and Jake returned to the car and got in. Brandon slid in close to Kari. His nearness started her pulse racing again. She couldn't let that happen, either.

Back at the parking lot, Brandon unlocked the car and he and Kari climbed inside. "So, what are you guys up to now?" Jake asked, leaning in the window on the driver's side.

"We thought we'd get some pizza," Brandon said.

Jake grinned. "Excellent! Mind if I tag along?"

Brandon turned to Kari with raised eyebrows. She shrugged helplessly, wishing she could strangle Jake on the spot.

"If you really want to," Brandon said. Kari noted that he didn't sound any more enthusiastic than she felt.

At the Pizza Palace, Jake insisted that he and Brandon share a pepperoni pizza, and Brandon bought Kari two slices with mushrooms. While they ate, Jake did most of the talking. He didn't even seem to notice their silence.

As soon as they had finished eating, Kari and Brandon left Jake talking with some of his friends. On the way to her house, Brandon apologized for Jake inviting himself along.

"He didn't exactly give us much choice," Kari said.

"You're right about that." Brandon turned into her street. "Jake's kind of pushy, but he's not a bad guy. We've been buddies for a long time."

After he pulled up in front of her house, Brandon cut the motor and put his hand on her arm. "Kari, I'm sorry about what happened tonight—the keys, Jake, everything. It sure fouled things up. We didn't even get a chance to talk."

Kari felt the warmth of his hand through the sleeve of her sweater. True, she hadn't told him about Dr. Evans, or about canceling his father's dinner invitation before it had been offered, but she could tell him all that another time.

Looking up at his face that was bathed in the glow of a streetlight, she smiled. "It's okay, really. I had a good time. And it certainly wasn't boring!"

Brandon moved closer to her, and Kari caught her breath. Was he going to kiss her? Maybe he thought she expected him to. He probably thought every girl he went out with wanted to be kissed. Well, he was wrong!

Abruptly, she moved away. "I have to go," she said, opening the car door. "Thanks for a nice time. See you Monday, I guess."

When the front door closed behind her, Kari leaned her head against it and sighed. She *had* wanted Brandon to kiss her. Then why hadn't she let him? Kari knew the answer very well: She was afraid she might have liked it too much.

After working in the student government office, Kari was late for lunch on Monday. She went through the cafeteria line and found Wendy, who had saved her a seat at their usual table.

"Brandon came by and asked where you were," Wendy told her. "He seemed *very* disappointed that you weren't here."

Kari felt a blush creep over her cheeks. She'd filled her friend in about most of Saturday night, but she hadn't said a word about her growing feelings for Brandon.

Wendy didn't miss the blush. "Hmmm. Very interesting."

Glancing over to where Brandon was sitting, Kari found him looking at her. When their eyes met, he grinned and waved, and Kari waved back.

"I think there's more than planning sessions going on here," Wendy said as she watched the exchange.

Kari picked up her sandwich. "Well, you're wrong. The only reason we're seeing each other so much is to figure out a way to break up our parents' romance."

Throughout lunch, whenever Kari stole a glance at Brandon, she caught him looking at her. Shortly before the bell rang, he came over to her table. Smiling, he said, "I missed you at your locker this morning."

"Look at the time!" Wendy said suddenly, picking up her tray. "I'd better get going. See you later, Kari." She hurried off, leaving Kari and Brandon alone.

Kari stood up, too, and began gathering her books. "I had an early meeting with the other class presidents. Was there something special you wanted to see me about?"

"Yeah," Brandon said. "I thought maybe we could study together for Friday's chemistry test after baseball practice today."

Kari's heart gave a little skip of pleasure. "That's a great idea," she said. "But I really can't. I have to go home and hang out by the phone." Then she explained the mistake she'd made about their parents' dinner date. "I sure goofed on that one," she added.

He shook his head. "It wasn't your fault. I thought he'd already asked her, too. And I guess you're right—he'll probably be calling her. Dad got home from his trip last night." The bell rang, and Brandon added, "Come on. I'll walk you to class."

They joined the crowd of students leaving the cafeteria. "Isn't your fourth period class over in the other wing?" Kari asked.

"Yeah," he said. "So I'll be a little late."

He left Kari at the door to her classroom, then strode off in the opposite direction. Kari walked slowly down the aisle to her seat, her mind in a whirl. How could she ever have thought Brandon was like that dumb football player and all the other athletes she'd known? He was nothing like them at all. In fact, he was nothing like any other boy Kari had ever met.

That night, Kari got lucky. Just before six, Mr. Duncan called. Kari told him her mom wasn't home. She asked him if she could take a message. Mr. Duncan hesitated. "I just wanted to invite her out for dinner on Saturday."

"Oh, that's too bad." Kari's mind began racing frantically to come up with an excuse. "We're—we're going camping!"

"Camping?"

Kari picked up on the distaste in his voice. Delighted, she said, "Oh, we love the outdoor thing. You know—hiking, tents, no running water, dirt."

After a long pause, Mr. Duncan said. "Oh. Well, I'll talk to her later."

When she hung up, Kari slumped into a chair. Now all she had to do was convince her mom to come along with her and Wendy's family—and that wasn't going to be easy!

Two days later, Kari headed for her chemistry class, hoping to have a few minutes to talk to Brandon. When she saw him up ahead walking with Jake, she hurried to catch up with them. She was about to say something, but they were deep in conversation, so she hung back. "We got to take that test Friday," she heard Jake saying.

Brandon sighed. "I can't believe he'd do that to us."

"With all these extra practices, I haven't had a chance to study at all," Jake said. "Have you got a copy?"

"You're in luck, my man. Here." Brandon reached into his notebook and handed Jake several pages stapled together.

Kari froze. Brandon was actually giving Jake the chemistry test! That was cheating!

She clenched her fists, staring after the boys as they walked away. She blinked back tears of anger and disappointment. She'd begun to think that Brandon was different, but he wasn't. Now she was convinced that he really was a dumb jock—and a cheater, too!

Chapter Nine

Early Sunday, Kari kicked open the side door of the garage and dumped her sleeping bag and duffel bag on the laundry table. It might have been a decent camping trip if her anger at Brandon hadn't spoiled everything. He'd tried to talk to her last week, but she'd refused to speak to him. And she'd studied extra hard to make sure that *she'd* do well on Friday's chemistry test.

Kari could still hardly believe Brandon had given Jake a copy of that test. She'd been right about him in the first place. She would never get involved with an athlete again, no matter how handsome and charming he was.

Before going into the house, Kari took her dirty laundry out of the duffel bag and started a load of wash. Everything sure got grungy on a camping trip—that was the part her mom didn't like. Kari's efforts to convince her to come along had been a dismal failure. No amount of coaxing had worked, so Kari had given up and gone without her, telling herself that if Mr. Duncan called while she was away, she'd worry about it later. Unfortunately, this *was* later.

Wondering what had happened, Kari went into the kitchen. She paused and sniffed. Something smelled delicious—like cookies baking. Just then the door to the dining room swung open.

"Gramma!" Kari cried, running to give her grandmother a hug. "What are you doing here?"

"Hi, sweetie. My, it's good to see you!" her grandmother said. Noticing Kari's puzzled expression, she added, "Did you forget about the conference your mother's attending in New Orleans?"

"Oh, yeah, I remember now. But doesn't it start tomorrow?"

Her grandmother pulled out a tray of chocolate chip cookies from the oven. "She decided to go down a day early and wanted me to be here when you got home from your camping trip. But I didn't expect you until this evening."

Kari took a carton of milk from the refrigerator and poured herself a tall glass. "The weather wasn't all that great. I guess we should have gone earlier in the year, before it got so hot and sticky."

Piling a handful of warm cookies on a napkin, Kari sat down at the kitchen table. "These are great, as usual," she said, popping a cookie into her mouth. It was always nice to see her grandmother, but now she'd have to wait until her mother came home to find out if Mr. Duncan had succeeded in inviting her to dinner.

"I'm glad your mom could get away for a day of relaxation before that big convention starts," her grandmother said. "And I really like that nice Mr. Duncan she went with. They seem to enjoy each other's company."

Kari choked on her cookie. There had to be some mistake! Her mother couldn't have gone off to New Orleans with Mr. Duncan! "You're sure the man's name was Duncan? *Chad* Duncan?"

"Yes, dear, I'm sure. He seemed like a delightful man, and it's nice that your mother didn't have to drive all by herself."

"Excuse me, Gramma!" Kari grabbed another cookie and dashed out of the kitchen and up the stairs to her bedroom. Her first impulse was to call Brandon, but since she was so mad at him, she decided to phone Wendy instead.

When her friend answered, Kari didn't even say hello. "Wendy, this is really *serious*," she wailed. "Gramma's here, and she says Mom went off to New Orleans with Mr. Duncan!"

Wendy gasped. "You don't think . . . ?"

"That's exactly what I *am* thinking." Kari collapsed on the bed. "I'm afraid they ran off to get married! Oh, Wendy, I've got to stop them!"

"It might be too late," Wendy said.

"But I have to try." Kari's stomach tightened in panic. "I'm going to New Orleans to find them. Can you get the car and drive me?"

"Sorry, but I can't. I'd like to, but my folks and I are going to my aunt and uncle's. We're just about to leave."

"Can't you get out of it?" Kari pleaded.

"No way. It's a family celebration for my aunt's birthday." Then she added, "Why don't you call Brandon? Maybe he could drive you."

"*Brandon?* You've got to be kidding!" Kari exclaimed. "I'd rather die!"

"Try to forget about what happened. For the moment anyway," Wendy suggested. "Brandon has a car, and he'll probably be just as upset as you are."

Reluctantly, Kari said, "I guess you're right."

"I've got to go," Wendy said. "Call him, okay?"

When she hung up, Kari stared at the phone a long time. She hated the thought of calling Brandon, and she hated the thought of riding to New Orleans with him even more. But how else could she get there?

Before dialing his number, Kari called her mother's hotel, but there was no listing for either a Mrs. Cortland or a Mr. Duncan. She groaned. Maybe they'd registered under fake names so she and Brandon couldn't track them down!

Kari gave up, realizing that she couldn't handle this alone. Gritting her teeth, she phoned Brandon. She wasn't surprised by the wariness in his voice. "Oh, so now you've decided to speak to me again," he said. "Are you going to let me know what's wrong?"

Kari ignored his question. "This is an emergency!"

"Oh, sure," Brandon scoffed.

Kari took a deep breath. "I think our parents might have gone off to get married."

"*What?*" Brandon yelled. "Where did you get that dumb idea?"

"We'll see how dumb it is. Did your dad go out of town today?"

"Yeah, on another business trip."

"Well, he went to New Orleans with *my mother*!" Kari's voice rose, but she couldn't seem to control it.

"Your mom tagged along with my dad?" Brandon sounded outraged. "She has a lot of nerve!"

"My mother has a conference in New Orleans. It was your father who tagged along with *her*!" Kari shouted. "What if they've run away to get married?"

There was silence on Brandon's end of the line. Finally he asked. "Do you really think they did?"

"I hope not, but I'm going to try and find them."

"Wait for me! I'll drive," Brandon said promptly. Before she could respond, he hung up.

After hanging up the phone, Kari changed her clothes and added a touch of makeup, wondering why she bothered. Then she hurried downstairs to tell her grandmother that she and Brandon were going out for a while.

The trip to New Orleans was awkward, to say the least. At first, neither Kari nor Brandon said a word. Kari stared out the window, pretending to be absorbed in the view while Brandon concentrated on his driving.

Finally Brandon broke the silence. "This is ridiculous. We can't spend a whole day together and not say anything."

"If your dad hadn't started dating my mom, we wouldn't have to spend *any* time together," Kari snapped.

Brandon gave her a quick glare. "Is it that painful? I wish he hadn't started seeing her, either. If he marries her, it'll just ruin everything again. Another woman won't be any better."

"Than what?"

"Never mind," Brandon muttered. "It's none of your business."

But Kari suddenly needed to know. "Brandon," she said, "what happened to your mom?"

Brandon's knuckles grew white as his hands clutched the steering wheel. "She left." He was obviously very bitter.

Kari had assumed his mother had died, as her father had. "When?" she asked softly.

Keeping his eyes on the road, Brandon didn't speak for a while. Finally he let out a long sigh. "She ran off when I was twelve. She wanted a singing career." He let out a short, humorless laugh. "Dad tried to get her to come back, but she wouldn't, so they got a divorce. She wasn't good enough for him, anyway."

Now Kari could see where his anger was coming from. She knew that there was no use in trying to persuade him that her mother wasn't anything like the woman who'd abandoned him. He wouldn't listen. Though her heart softened toward Brandon, she couldn't forgive him for cheating. Once they found their parents and hopefully prevented them from getting married, Kari would have nothing further to do with him.

"What hotel is your mother staying at?" Brandon asked when they arrived in New Orleans.

"The Royal Sonesta in the French Quarter," she answered.

"Oh, terrific," he said. "We'll never find them in the Quarter."

But Kari refused to become depressed. "Let's see if she's checked in yet."

Brandon inched along in heavy traffic and pulled up in front of a pink hotel laced with black wrought-iron balconies.

"I'll run in," Kari told him. "You can drive around the block. Just don't go off without me," she added as she slammed the door.

She asked the desk clerk if her mother had checked in. He couldn't find a reservation for Elizabeth Cortland or for Chad Duncan.

Waiting on the curb for Brandon, Kari soaked up the atmosphere of old New Orleans where she and her mother had visited many times before. She loved the French Quarter with its narrow streets and intricate ironwork balconies. The houses with their shuttered windows lent a mysterious air to the area. Kari had always liked to imagine all the things that might be going on behind those shutters.

Brandon honked the horn, and Kari jumped in beside him before the traffic began to move again. "They're not registered," she told him. "I guess we could hang around here in case they come, but they might not check in until late tonight."

"Especially if they have something more important to do," Brandon muttered grimly.

Kari shuddered. "Don't say that! What if we're too late?"

"Well, let's drive around a little." Brandon joined the stream of traffic. "Maybe they're sightseeing in the Quarter."

Kari leaned forward and peered out the window. "Start on Royal Street. My mom always likes to go there."

As Brandon drove slowly down streets crowded with tourists window-shopping at antique storefronts and wandering in and out of many quaint gift shops, Kari strained to look everywhere.

Half an hour later she admitted to failure. "This is going to be impossible. Even if they're here, we'd never be able to pick them out of the crowd."

Brandon turned the car down Bourbon Street, and Kari suddenly grabbed his arm. "Look! Up ahead! That's my mom's gray car!"

Giving her a disgusted look, he said, "Yeah, right. There must be a million gray cars."

"I saw it as we rounded the corner. It's got to be hers," Kari insisted. "I saw part of the license number!"

Reluctantly, Brandon admitted she could be right. "Try to keep it in sight then."

"They're making a right at the next stop sign," Kari cried.

He flipped on his right-turn signal, then glanced in the rearview mirror. "Uh-oh. We've got trouble," he said as a mounted policeman rode up behind them, motioning Brandon to pull over. "At least we know it's not a speeding ticket," Brandon added as he rolled down his window.

"I can't *believe* this," Kari moaned and slumped against the seat. "Now we'll lose them for sure!"

The policeman dismounted and asked to see Brandon's driver's license. He studied it a minute and handed it back. "Do you know you have a brake light out?" he asked.

Brandon let out a sigh. "No officer, I didn't."

"Go get it fixed right now," the officer said. Then he mounted his horse and rode away.

Brandon collapsed over the steering wheel. "We're lucky he didn't give me a ticket."

Kari covered her face with her hands. "A brake light! We lost my mom for a stupid *brake light!*"

"Remember, we're hunting for my dad, too." Brandon eased the car away from the curb. "I'd better get a new bulb before we're stopped again."

After a quick trip to an auto parts store, he replaced the broken light. "How about a break? My stomach's growling like a bear

100

after a long winter," he said as he climbed back into the car.

Kari realized that she was hungry, too. "Let's go to the French Market and have *beignets*. I love those French doughnuts, and so does Mom. Maybe she and your father went there."

"Sounds great to me—*if* we can find a parking place."

After two trips through the market, they found a spot near the Cafe du Monde.

"Inside or out?" Brandon asked.

"Outside," she said. "We can keep a better eye out for our parents if they come along."

After the waiter set the plates of powdered-sugar-covered doughnuts in front of them and handed them steaming mugs of *café au lait*, Kari sipped her mixture of half coffee, half hot milk, scanning the face of every passerby.

Brandon devoured his plate of doughnuts in record time and asked for another order while Kari was still finishing hers. As she bit into one, she inhaled some of the powdered sugar and started coughing. Brandon leaned over and pounded her on the back. "That sugar's murder when you breathe it. Are you okay?"

She nodded and took a sip of *café au lait*. Over the rim of her mug, she saw Brandon grinning at her. "What's so funny?" she asked, frowning.

"Your face."

"Well, gee, thanks." Kari drew back. "How come you never mentioned it before?"

Laughing, he replied, "You never looked like you fell in a flour sack before!"

Grabbing her napkin, Kari rubbed at her cheeks.

"Here—let me do it." Gently Brandon wiped away the remaining sugar. His face was very close to hers, and she could feel his breath on her cheek. For some crazy reason, her heart started pounding.

Abruptly, she pulled away. "That's fine, thanks. I can get the rest," she said stiffly.

His eyes narrowed. "Kari, what's wrong? Lately you've been acting like I'm an ax murderer or something."

She turned away and studied the people walking past them. Finally she mumbled, "I don't like cheaters."

"I don't either." He sounded puzzled. "So who's cheating?"

"Don't play games! You know you gave Jake that test."

Brandon stared at her. "What test? What are you talking about?"

"The chemistry test we had on Friday. I heard Jake ask you for a copy, and you gave it to him. That's cheating!"

Taken aback, Brandon shook his head. "I don't have any idea what—" He broke off, and Kari could see it was finally dawning on him.

102

To her surprise, a slow smile crossed Brandon's face. "I *did* give Jake a copy of a test last week. Now don't get all icy on me again. Let me explain."

Kari waited, wondering what kind of an explanation he'd come up with.

He took her hand. "Jake and I had a test for *baseball* on Friday. The coach wanted to make sure we knew all the rules inside and out, and he passed out the questions so we'd know what to study. I just gave Jake my sample copy to look over."

Kari caught her breath. "You mean . . . oh, I feel so stupid!" She had never wanted to believe that Brandon was capable of cheating. Now she'd made a fool of herself. She wanted to slide under the table and hide. "I really thought it was happening all over again," she whispered.

"What was happening?" Brandon asked. When he insisted, Kari told him about the cheating episode with the football player.

"No wonder you were all bent out of shape," he said when she had finished. "Honest, Kari, I'm not like him."

Too embarrassed to meet his gaze, Kari looked away. And then out of the corner of her eye, she saw a familiar print dress at the top of the levee. "There they are," she exclaimed. "That's my mom's new sundress!"

Chapter Ten

"Hurry, Brandon!" Kari called as she headed up to the Moonwalk that ran along the top of the levee through River Park. "I *know* I saw them!"

Brandon threw some money on the table and chased after her. Catching up, he jogged beside her. "Are you sure it's them?" he asked between breaths.

She panted. "It sure *looked* like them. I recognized the dress. She just bought it."

Brandon grabbed her hand. "Okay, let's go get 'em," he said, pulling her along as they raced to the top of the levee. "We don't want to lose them this time."

When they paused to catch their breath,

Kari realized that Brandon hadn't let go of her hand. She decided that she was glad.

Two blocks ahead, she caught a glimpse of the woman in the brightly colored sundress and the man beside her. She pointed down the Moonwalk. "There they are!"

Hand in hand, they ran along the walkway, dodging around more leisurely strollers. As they got closer, Kari called out, "Mom! Wait up!"

When the couple ahead didn't react, she shouted again, "*Mom!* It's me, Kari—and Brandon!" Mrs. Cortland still didn't turn around, and Kari noticed how intent she was on Mr. Duncan. Too intent to recognize her own daughter's voice. Apparently love was not only blind—it was deaf, too!

Brandon began calling his dad as they closed the distance between them. When they were just a few yards away, he yelled, "Come on, Dad! You can't pretend you don't hear us."

Then the couple turned, and Kari and Brandon stopped short. It wasn't Mrs. Cortland and Mr. Duncan. It was a woman wearing a dress like Mrs. Cortland's and a dark-haired man in a tan suit.

Embarrassed, Kari babbled, "We're sorry—we thought you were our parents. You look exactly like them—I mean, from the back. . . ."

The couple laughed, and the woman said, "That's perfectly all right. Hope you find them."

Brandon shook his head as they watched the man and the woman in the sundress continue along the Moonwalk. "That's really weird. From behind he looked just like my dad."

Dropping onto a bench, they tried to decide what to do next. "Since this is going to take longer than I thought, I'd better call Gramma and tell her where we are. She probably thinks we're at a movie in the mall or something," Kari said.

At a much slower speed, Kari and Brandon retraced their steps to the Cafe du Monde and found a phone booth. After Kari made her call, she rejoined Brandon, shaking her head. "Mom called about an hour ago. She's *delighted* we went out together!" Kari rolled her eyes.

"Did she say anything about changing hotels?" Brandon asked.

Kari sighed. "Not a word. Let's go back to the Royal Sonesta," she suggested. "That's where Mom was supposed to be."

"How about if we get something else to eat first? I'm starving," Brandon announced. "Everything around here costs about a month's worth of allowances. Why don't we find some fast food outside the Quarter?"

"Okay, but let's hurry. We've got to get back and try to find them." Kari looked out the window. "I just hope we're not too late," she whispered.

When they found a hamburger place and went inside, Kari realized she had no idea if she had enough money. Turning her back to Brandon, she pulled out her wallet to see what she could afford to order. It didn't look like it was going to be much, so she ordered a small hamburger.

Brandon was surprised. "No fries, no drink?"

"This is fine," Kari assured him. "I'm kind of short on cash."

"Hey, I'll buy," he offered.

"No." She shook her head. "You paid for my *beignets*."

Brandon told her to find a table while he waited for their orders. When he joined her, Kari saw that he had gotten two double cheeseburgers, two fries, and two large sodas. He put one of each in front of her. Kari started to protest, but Brandon just said, "My treat, okay?"

Kari smiled. "Okay. Thanks!"

They ate in silence. Just before they were ready to go, Kari said, "Brandon, tell me something." She hesitated, wondering if she should go on, then decided she might as well. "Why do all the guys call you 'Bubba'?"

Brandon grinned at her. "Why? Don't you like it?"

"Well, it's just—it makes you sound . . ." Kari floundered.

"Dorky?" Brandon suggested. "I hate it, too." He started laughing.

Kari said, "Well then, why . . . ?"

"Jake started calling me Bubba after a famous football player when we first started playing football back in grade school. It just sort of caught on, and I never did anything about it. Maybe it's time I did."

Kari laughed, too. "I think maybe you're right. Brandon's really a very nice name."

"Thanks," he said. "Okay, Slave Driver. Now that we've satisfied the old appetite, we can get back to tracing our problem parents."

"Let's check the Royal Sonesta one more time," Kari said. "Maybe Mom has checked in by now."

They got into the car and headed back to the French Quarter. When they reached the hotel, Kari went inside again. She discovered that a new desk clerk had come on duty. Giving him her mother's name, she watched him call up the computer listings. "No one registered by that name, miss."

Kari swallowed hard. "Try Duncan then." She crossed her fingers, hoping her mother wasn't registered under Mr. Duncan's name. That could mean only one thing . . . married.

"Nothing there either." The desk clerk leaned

forward, and spoke in a fatherly manner. "Honey, are you sure your mother was planning to stay here?"

"Yes—she's attending the convention that starts tomorrow."

His face lit up. "Then she might be listed under the company."

Kari hadn't thought of that. She gave him the name of her mom's company, and he turned back to the computer. "Here it is— Clarkson Products. I have a Cortland listed."

"Is it a single or a double?" Kari asked anxiously.

"A single. She's all checked in."

"Oh, thank you, sir! Thank you *so* much," Kari exclaimed. She raced out of the hotel, almost knocking over a bellboy coming in with a cart full of luggage.

Seeing Brandon double-parked in front of the hotel, she ran over to him. "I found Mom's registration!" she shouted.

"Are she and my dad there?" he asked.

"I'll try to find out while you get a parking place."

Kari hurried back into the hotel and located the house phone. "*Please* be here," she whispered. But after the phone had rung ten times, she reluctantly hung up.

A few minutes later, Brandon came into the lobby. "Any luck?" he asked.

Kari shook her head. "No one's in the

room. We'll just have to stay here and wait for them."

"That could take all night." He sank down into one of the lobby couches.

Kari sat down beside him. "If only they haven't gotten married," she sighed.

"I just can't believe my dad would do anything as stupid as that," Brandon mumbled.

She jerked upright, eyes blazing. "Marrying my mother would not be stupid! The *really* stupid thing was her getting involved with your dad in the first place!"

Brandon glared at her. "You've really got things mixed up."

"You bet I did. I came here with you, didn't I?" Kari snapped. Jumping up from the couch, she marched over to the main entrance and stood with her back to Brandon, staring outside. He really wasn't nice at all! And she would be stuck with him for a long time—they still had to ride home together. But after that, Kari promised herself she'd ignore him for life!

Half an hour later, she picked up the house phone and called her mother's room again. There was still no answer. On her way back to the door, she glanced into the lounge—and stopped short. There at a small table sat her mom, laughing at something Mr. Duncan was saying.

Kari raced over to them. "Mom! How can

110

you just sit here laughing when we've spent the whole day looking for you?"

Mrs. Cortland and Mr. Duncan looked up at her in amazement. "Kari, what on earth are you doing here?" her mother said.

"We came to find you. And to stop you!" Kari announced, just as Brandon came into the lounge.

"Dad! You didn't do it, did you?" he asked his father.

Mr. Duncan stared from Kari to Brandon, obviously confused. "Do what? What are you talking about, son?"

"You didn't *marry* her, did you? We don't need her! She'll just leave like—" Brandon broke off.

"Where did you get that idea?" his father asked incredulously.

"Well, we thought—"

Kari interrupted. "You ran off together. We were afraid you might be up to something— like marriage."

"We didn't want you to do anything dumb," Brandon added, slumping into a chair next to his father.

"Kari, sit down," Mrs. Cortland said sternly, pointing to the chair next to her. Kari sat. "We did not 'run off,' and there was never any question of marriage. You knew I was going to the convention."

"Yes, but not with *him*," Kari said, frowning.

"That's enough. Mr. Duncan simply came with me so we could enjoy a day in the French Quarter. He's going on a business trip tonight."

Mr. Duncan held up his right hand. "On my honor as a former Boy Scout, I fly to Chicago at nine o'clock," he said solemnly.

"Now about this marriage nonsense . . ." Mrs. Cortland began. She and Mr. Duncan explained how they felt about each other. In turn, Brandon and Kari told their parents how strongly they objected to their relationship.

"I knew our friendship had upset you," Mrs. Cortland said when Kari had finished, "but I had no idea how much. We'll talk more about it when I get back from this convention." She sighed. "Perhaps I *have* been seeing Chad too often. . . ."

An hour later, Kari and Brandon were on their way home. Kari sat rigidly on her side of the front seat, thinking that if she and Brandon had really succeeded in breaking up their parents' romance, she wouldn't have to see him anymore.

"Looks like our mission might be accomplished," he said.

Kari nodded, stifling a yawn. "I hope so."

Brandon glanced at her. "Tired? You can put your head on my shoulder if you like."

"No. I'm fine." Kari wasn't going to rest her

head on his shoulder, no matter how worn-out she was.

"It's pretty exhausting, keeping up with parents, isn't it?" Brandon murmured. And when he reached out and pulled her close to his side, Kari didn't resist.

Chapter Eleven

For the next several days, Brandon and Kari saw each other at school, but there was no reason for them to get together, and no further plans to be made. They were waiting for their parents to come home to find out if they had really broken up.

A few times Brandon started to come over to her in the halls, but something always seemed to happen. Once, they'd even begun to talk, but Jake had butted in with some of his corny jokes. Another time at lunch, Brandon had walked toward her and Wendy's table, then hesitated and changed course, joining a group of baseball players instead.

Kari had to admit that she missed Brandon—she'd gotten used to meeting him every day. And whenever she thought about their movie date, or the comfortable feeling she'd had snuggled next to him on the trip back from New Orleans, she wished they could get together again. It seemed a lifetime ago since Kari had thought he was a dumb jock and a cheater.

When Kari got home from school on Thursday afternoon, her mother and grandmother were sitting at the kitchen table having a cup of coffee.

Kari ran to her mom and hugged her tightly. "I'm so glad to have you back," she said, not sure if she meant from the convention or from Mr. Duncan.

Mrs. Cortland smiled. "It's good to be back, honey. The conference went well, but I missed you." Rusty looked up from where he lay at her feet and whimpered. "And you, too," she added.

Kari's grandmother poured a glass of milk for her and offered her some cookies.

When Kari sat down at the table, Mrs. Cortland said quietly, "Before you ask, Kari, I want you to know that Mr. Duncan and I have decided not to see each other for a while."

Gramma frowned. "Elizabeth, are you sure . . . ?"

"We agreed that we couldn't ignore the feelings of both our kids."

"Oh, Mom, I'm so glad!" Kari exclaimed.

"Now we can have our Sundays together again, and I won't have to eat alone anymore."

"I'm glad *you're* glad. We'll plan something nice for Sunday while we drive your grandmother home."

Leaning over, Kari kissed her grandmother. "You'll fill the cookie jar before you leave, won't you, Gramma?"

Her grandmother smiled. "That's a promise!"

The following morning, Brandon met Kari at her locker. Grinning, he held out his hand. "Congratulations, partner!"

Kari shook his extended hand and felt a familiar tingle at his touch. "Mom told me they'd decided not to see each other for the time being," she said.

"Yeah, my dad said the same thing." Slowly he released her hand. "He said it was because it matters so much to me."

"I guess we're pretty lucky to have parents that pay attention to our feelings," Kari said.

"Yeah. Hey, feel like celebrating? We could catch a soda after school. I don't have practice today."

"I can't," Kari said regretfully. "There's a meeting for anyone planning to run for office next year."

"You running for senior class president?"

"I'm going to try."

"Well, you've got my vote," Brandon said.

Then suddenly he slapped his forehead. "Oh, brother! I just remembered that I couldn't have gone either. I promised to take this kid I'm tutoring out for pizza."

Kari's eyes widened. "You tutor somebody?"

"Usually just on Saturday afternoon," he said. "But this time's special. He actually got a *B* on a test."

As Brandon left, Kari watched him until he disappeared into the throng of students. So that was what he did on Saturdays! And here she'd just assumed he was playing some dumb sport. Kari was finding out more and more about Brandon, and she definitely liked what she was learning.

After driving Kari's grandmother to her house in False River, a town on the Mississippi River north of Baton Rouge, Kari's mother said, "I thought we'd stop at Roussel's for crayfish on the way home. They're still in season."

Kari's mouth watered. "I'd love it! It's so great to be doing something together on Sunday again."

"I'm looking forward to it, too," Mrs. Cortland said. But Kari thought her mother didn't really seem very happy.

During the next few days, Kari noticed a difference in her mom. She hardly ever smiled, and she didn't sing anymore. It was almost like the year Kari's father had died. Surely Mr. Duncan didn't mean that much to her—did he?

At first, Kari had been thrilled to have her mother's company for dinner every night. But it wasn't as much fun as she had anticipated. Mrs. Cortland seemed preoccupied. She didn't have much to say, and Kari had to provide most of the conversation.

Bit by bit, an uneasy feeling crept over her. Her mother obviously wasn't happy. The spark was gone, and it was all Kari's fault. She'd been thinking only of herself when she'd been so eager to break up the romance with Mr. Duncan. She hadn't considered her mother's feelings at all.

"I've really been so selfish," she whispered to Rusty one evening as Mrs. Cortland sat in the living room watching TV. "I love Mom so much, but all I've done is make her miserable. If only there was some way I could make up for it. . . ."

And then things took a sudden turn for the better. Checking the answering machine when she got home from school, Kari discovered a message from her mother saying that she would be home late because she was going to dinner with Dr. Evans.

Kari let out a whoop. Grabbing her little dog, she whirled him around. "Rusty! You did it! If you hadn't gotten that foxtail in your ear, Mom wouldn't have had to take you to the vet, and Dr. Evans wouldn't have asked her out!" She danced around the room. "Maybe this will cheer her up," she told Rusty. "It certainly makes *me* feel a whole lot better!"

At ten o'clock, Kari put the kettle on the stove so she would have tea ready when her mother returned, thinking, *She must be having a good time if she's still at dinner.* Kari remembered the last time she'd waited up for her mother. It had been Mrs. Cortland's first date with Mr. Duncan, and Kari had been dying of curiosity, just as she was now.

Fifteen minutes later, Mrs. Cortland came in and collapsed into an overstuffed chair in the living room. "I'm exhausted!" she groaned.

Kari handed her a cup of tea. "I guess you liked Dr. Evans—you stayed so long."

"I stayed because he never stopped talking." Her mother sat up so she could handle the cup. "He kept going on and on about the same things. All he could talk about was his clinic. I heard about sick dogs, sick cats, even a pelican with a split beak!"

Kari drooped, all hope gone. "Pretty boring, huh?"

"With a capital *B*," her mother agreed.

"That's too bad," Kari said. "I really thought he'd be great—he's *so* attractive."

Mrs. Cortland smiled. "I'll give you that. Dr. Evans is a very good-looking man. It just goes to show what I always tell you—beauty is only skin deep. But some people are beautiful inside."

Kari wondered if her mom thought Mr. Duncan was beautiful inside. Maybe he was, but Kari had never bothered to find out. She didn't know what to say, so she just kissed her mother and trudged upstairs to bed.

At school the next day, Kari sought Brandon out before chemistry class. "How are things going at home?" she asked.

He shrugged. "Okay, I guess. My dad isn't very good company, though. He eats in front of the TV or works all night. We used to talk a lot, but now he seems sort of out of it."

Kari sighed. "Yeah, I know what you mean. It's the same with my mom."

Brandon sat down on the edge of his desk. "I didn't think they'd be so unhappy."

"I didn't either," Kari said, "but I'm afraid that's what's happened."

Brandon gave her a hopeful look. "Maybe they'll get over it."

"I hope so," Kari said. She caught sight of Jake and two of Brandon's other friends coming into the classroom, so she said goodbye and went to her seat. Maybe Brandon was right. Maybe it was only temporary.

But she didn't really think it was. On Saturday morning, Kari went to Wendy's house when she was sure her friend would be home from her modeling class.

"Wendy, I need to talk to someone about my mom," she said. "She's really miserable, and it's just eating me up inside."

"I've got all afternoon. Let's get a cold drink," Wendy said, leading the way to the kitchen.

After pouring two sodas, the girls went upstairs and settled themselves in the middle of Wendy's bed. "Okay, I'm listening," Wendy said as she leaned against the headboard.

Kari stretched out beside her. "I'm afraid I've ruined Mom's life."

"Don't be so melodramatic. You couldn't have . . ."

The phone on the bedside table rang, and Wendy picked up the receiver. "Hello? . . . Yes, this is she . . ." A frown crossed her face and she bit her lip. "Just a minute." She put her hand over the mouthpiece.

Kari rolled to a sitting position. "Who is it?"

"It's the lady from the modeling agency. She has another *opportunity* for me," Wendy whispered. "I'm sick of being *chosen* to hand out samples or make babies smile! Help me get out of it."

"What can I do?" Kari asked.

"Just remind me of something else I have to do, and say it *loud*." Wendy spoke into the receiver. "I'm sorry—what was it you were saying?"

As Wendy listened intently, Kari watched her expression change, trying to judge when she should break in. Deciding that now was as good a time as any, she shouted, "Hey, Wendy! Don't forget you're all booked up next week."

Wendy waved frantically as she listened, and Kari decided that meant she wanted more. She might as well give it her best shot. "Wendy, *please* get off the phone," she said in a "motherly" bellow.

Wendy gave her a horrified look and madly motioned her to shut up as she scrambled off the bed and took the phone over to her desk. "No, no—it's nothing. I'll definitely be able to make it."

Realizing that she'd misread Wendy's signals, Kari flopped back on the bed. She hoped she hadn't ruined everything. But looking at her friend's animated expression, she decided that things were fine.

Hanging up, Wendy jumped up and down and shrieked, "I got an assignment! This one's for real!" She grabbed her pillow and started pounding Kari with it.

"Help!" Kari giggled. She snatched the pillow. "Calm down and tell me about it."

Wendy hugged herself ecstatically. "They want me at a photo shoot *this afternoon*!

They're actually going to take pictures of *me*! Not babies—*me*!"

"That's fabulous!" Kari exclaimed. "I'm so happy for you. But what's the catch this time?"

"Well . . ." Wendy hesitated. "They want me to model preteen clothes." Both girls burst into laughter. "I don't care," Wendy said. "It's a start."

"And if you ever grow up," Kari said with a grin, "you can wear *big people* clothes!"

"Stop it!" Wendy reached for the pillow again but Kari grabbed it.

"Really, Wendy, this is terrific news."

Wendy sat up. "I almost forgot. What were you saying about your mom?"

Kari just couldn't dump all her troubles on her friend when she was so happy and excited. "It's okay. I'll tell you about it after the photo session."

"Are you sure? You seemed pretty upset."

"I'm sure," Kari smiled. "Now go knock 'em dead! I'm out of here."

Later that afternoon, Kari sprawled across her bed, unable to settle down to doing anything. She had another English paper to start, but she couldn't focus on it. Even the thought of reading a good book didn't interest her. She rolled over and stared at the ceiling. If only she could stop worrying about her mom.

Kari had offered to join her for the weekly grocery shopping, but Mrs. Cortland said she had a long list of other errands and Kari would be bored. And when her mother had returned, she'd started cleaning the basement, the way she always did when she was upset.

Glancing at the phone, Kari was strongly tempted to call Brandon. After all, he was as concerned about his father as she was about her mother. It wouldn't hurt to find out how Mr. Duncan was doing.

The phone rang six times before Brandon picked it up. "Hi," she said. "This is Kari. Uh—I was just wondering if there's anything new with your dad."

"Not really. Is something wrong?" he asked. "You sound funny."

"Oh, everything is horrible here," Kari said. "If I had only known how badly this would hurt Mom—well, maybe we should have left them alone."

"I've been thinking the same thing," Brandon admitted.

"We had no right to try to control their lives."

Brandon was silent for a moment. "I know. Can we fix it? Do you think we could turn things around?"

Kari sat up straight, her eyes sparkling with excitement. "We sure could try! We broke them up—maybe we can bring them back together!"

"Yeah. Why not?" Brandon sounded excited, too. "But we'll need to come up with a really good plan. Why don't I pick you up tomorrow so we can talk about it?"

"Oh, I'd love it," Kari said, "but I can't. Sunday's my special day with Mom, and now that she's so bummed, it's more important than ever."

"Then it'll have to be after baseball practice Monday. Let's meet at the Pizza Palace, okay?"

"Okay," Kari murmured. It wasn't a date, but at least it was a chance to be with him. "See you in chem class."

Just before Brandon hung up, he said softly, "And you know, Kari, maybe we could try again, too."

She stared at the phone. What did he mean by that? Did he only mean trying to get their parents back together? With all her heart, Kari hoped he meant something a lot more personal.

Chapter Twelve

In the student government office after school on Monday, Kari looked at her watch a hundred times while she helped to make campaign posters. Finally, it was time to meet Brandon. She decided to wait for him outside the locker room door so they could walk to the Pizza Palace together.

Brandon was the first one out of the locker room. He looked surprised and pleased to see her there. "Come on," he said, grabbing her hand. "Let's get out of here before Jake horns in." He started running down the hall, pulling Kari along.

"I'm sure he'd have a lot of ideas," she said, laughing as she tried to keep up with him.

"Yeah, all of them bad."

They hurried out of the school and down the street to the pizza parlor. They sat at the same table in the back corner, where they'd sat before. To Kari, that seemed like a lifetime ago. Then, they had been working so hard to break up their parents, and now they were trying to undo what they'd done.

Brandon got them each a soda and a slice. "Mushrooms, right?" he said. "I told them to pile 'em on."

"Yum!" Kari eyed the mound of mushrooms appreciatively. "You must know somebody in the kitchen."

"A guy from the football team," he mumbled around a mouthful of pepperoni-packed pizza.

Kari wondered if he'd forgotten why they were meeting. It would be so nice to go somewhere together without any business to take care of, just because they liked each other. But today that wasn't the case. "Have you come up with any ideas?" she asked.

Brandon grinned. "For 'Operation Patchup'?"

Kari nodded. "Do you really think we can do it?"

"Hope so," he said between bites. "And fast. Then we can have some time for ourselves."

Kari caught her breath. Was it possible to dream about a future for the two of them? She smiled shyly. "I'd like that."

"I think we ought to play up the romance angle," Brandon said. "What do you think is romantic?"

"Well . . . flowers," Kari told him. "Flowers are *very* romantic."

"Okay. I'll send some to your mom and sign my dad's name. What kind of flowers does she like?"

"Roses," Kari said. "Red roses. They're her favorites—and mine, too."

"What about that restaurant you said was so romantic, the one they didn't go to before?" Brandon asked.

"You mean La Cherie?"

"That's the one. And there's going to be a full moon in a few days."

Kari's eyes widened in surprise. "How do you know that?"

"I looked it up." Brandon grinned sheepishly. "I've been doing some research since I spoke to you on Saturday. I figure if Dad sends her flowers and takes her out to dinner at a romantic restaurant under a full moon, they'll be back together in no time flat."

"Sounds good," Kari admitted. "But how do we get them to the restaurant?"

For the next hour, as they worked out all the details of a romantic evening for their parents, Kari kept wishing that she and Brandon could share such a night. But she brushed that thought aside, reminding herself, *First things first.*

Kari could hardly wait for the end of the week so they could put their plan into action. They'd decided not to begin too early so there wouldn't be a lot of time for telephone conversations. Mr. Duncan was out of town again, but if he came home early, they could have a problem.

Shortly after Mrs. Cortland arrived home Thursday, the doorbell rang. "Can you get that, Kari?" she called.

Pretending she didn't hear, Kari slipped into the dining room where she could keep an eye on the door.

A moment later, Mrs. Cortland answered the bell. When the delivery man handed her a huge arrangement of red roses, she gasped. "Oh, my . . . they're beautiful!"

Kari stayed hidden while her mom brought the flowers to the living room and set them on the coffee table. Then she watched Mrs. Cortland read the card. When she smiled and held it to her cheek, Kari knew that Step One of the plan was a success. After a few more minutes, she came into the room. "Mom, what gorgeous flowers!" she exclaimed.

Mrs. Cortland said softly, "They're from Chad." She looked up at Kari as if she was anxious about her reaction.

"Red roses. He sure has good taste."

Mrs. Cortland hurried to the kitchen, and Kari heard her dialing the phone. She held her breath. Brandon should be picking it up on the other end any minute now.

"Oh, he's not there?" Her mother sounded disappointed. "I just wanted to thank him for the lovely flowers."

Kari knew exactly what Brandon was saying—if he kept to the script. He was promising to pass the message on to his dad. Kari grinned. They'd gotten over the first hurdle. Now for Step Two.

The next day Kari sat with Brandon at lunchtime. They compared notes on what had happened yesterday and exchanged the invitations they'd written to their parents. Kari had painstakingly copied her mother's writing onto a scented note card. Mr. Duncan shouldn't have any reason to think it wasn't the real thing. Brandon had scrawled his invitation in a fair imitation of his father's bold handwriting.

As soon as she got home, Kari slipped Brandon's note into her mom's stack of mail. Now she just had to wait.

When Mrs. Cortland arrived, she took off her suit jacket and absentmindedly picked up the mail. Kari tried to seem uninterested, but inside she was tied up in nervous knots, wondering how her mother would react to the note. Kari knew by heart the words she and Brandon had decided on:

Dear Elizabeth,
I'm getting into town early Saturday evening. It's time we got together again. Can you meet me at La Cherie at 8:00? I've missed you more than I can say.

Chad

Kari and Brandon had changed the time twice before agreeing on eight o'clock. It would be dark by then, and the full moon would just be beginning to rise.

Kari's smile reflected her mother's when she finished reading the invitation. It looked as if everything was falling into place. At this point, Kari and Brandon's only worry was the possibility of either parent phoning the other.

By Saturday night, even though Mr. Duncan hadn't called, Kari was a nervous wreck. In her mind, she ticked off the details that she and Brandon had already handled. They'd called La Cherie, making a reservation for two at a window table overlooking the river, and ordered a bottle of imported champagne. Brandon was dropping off a note at the restaurant explaining what they had done, to be delivered to their parents after they were seated.

If only we could be there to see how it all turns out, Kari thought.

The phone rang, and Kari picked it up in midring, hoping it wasn't Mr. Duncan.

"Kari?" She recognized Brandon's voice and sighed with relief. "Everything okay?" he asked.

"All set on this end. But you scared me to death! I thought it was your dad."

"Sorry about that." He chuckled. "Aren't you dying to know how it's going to turn out?"

"I was just wishing we could be there," she confessed.

"Don't you dare suggest we hide under the next table."

Kari giggled. "I can just see the waiter's face if we poked our heads out from under the tablecloth to place our order!"

"I wasn't thinking of anything that obvious, but I *was* thinking that maybe we could kind of check on them from outside," Brandon said. "You know, to make sure they got together."

"Brandon, that's brilliant!" Kari cried. "But we'd have to be very careful so that they don't see *us*."

"They'll never know we're there," he said.

"Let's do it!" After arranging to call Brandon as soon as her mom had left, Kari hung up and raced upstairs to change into a sundress and white flats. She could hardly wait for her mother to get going so she and Brandon could check the progress of "Operation Patchup."

It was a few minutes after eight when Brandon's car turned in at the sign announcing the French restaurant. Kari had only been there once before, and she was slightly overwhelmed by the tall trees that lined each side of the driveway, forming an oak alley. She gazed at the large white building with pillars across the front—La Cherie had once been a plantation home. Bougainvillea bushes heavy with dark pink blossoms surrounded the house and lined the wooden walkway along the river's edge. It was a romantic spot, all right, the perfect place to get their parents back together.

Brandon pulled into the parking lot. Before he and Kari got out, he took a shopping bag from the backseat.

"You plan to *shop* here?" Kari teased. "What's in the bag?"

"Secrets," he said with a mysterious smile, and he refused to tell her anything more.

As they approached the restaurant, Kari warned, "Not too close."

Brandon looked around. "See those bushes over there? If we sneak behind them, we can get a good view."

"Okay, Agent A. Lead on."

Casually they strolled across the moonlit lawn toward the shrubbery, as if they were just out for an evening walk. When they reached the bushes, they quickly scurried into the shadows and edged around the building until they had a good view of the window tables on the riverside.

Kari clutched Brandon's arm. "Brandon, there they are—in the corner!" she whispered.

"And here comes the note we wrote," he whispered back as the waiter presented Mr. Duncan with an envelope. "We're just in time."

They watched Brandon's father read the message and hand it to Kari's mother. "He's smiling!" Kari said, waiting anxiously for her mom's reaction.

Then Mrs. Cortland smiled, too, and looked into Mr. Duncan's eyes, her face glowing. As Mr. Duncan reached for her mom's hand, Kari and Brandon beamed at each other. "I think we pulled it off," she said.

Brandon nodded. "We're getting pretty good at this. I don't think we need to stay any longer. Come on." He took her hand and led her down to the wooden walkway along the river. The full moon dominated the dark sky, bathing them in its soft glow.

"Where are we going?" Kari whispered, but she didn't really care. As long as Brandon held her hand, she'd walk forever.

His smile widened. "We have to eat, too."

Stepping off the boardwalk, he sat down on the grassy bank next to it, pulling her down beside him. "I wish we could have gone to someplace nice," he said. "But after this romantic interlude," he nodded toward the restaurant, "I've used up all my available cash, so I brought Chinese. It's probably ice-cold by now."

Kari laughed, thinking of her own depleted allowance. "I'm crazy about cold Chinese."

Brandon opened his shopping bag and produced several white take-out containers, a package of birthday candles, and a box of matches. Then he took out a single red rose. "You said you thought flowers were romantic, too."

Speechless with delight, Kari pressed the rose to her cheek. No one had ever given her flowers before. She knew she'd rather have this one perfect blossom than her mother's whole bouquet. Brandon never ceased to amaze her. *Just think what I might have missed if Mr. Duncan hadn't started dating my mom,* she thought.

Opening the package of candles, Brandon wedged each one into a narrow crack between two planks in the boardwalk. Then he lit them until a row of tiny flames flickered beside them. "How's that for a candlelit meal?"

Kari didn't know if she was going to laugh

or cry. In her whole life, she was sure there would never be a more romantic dinner. "It's perfect," she murmured.

He leaned over and gently brushed her lips with his. His hand twined in Kari's hair, pulling her closer as the kiss deepened and ignited a spark within her.

Releasing her briefly, Brandon blew out the candles, then took her in his arms. "We don't want to catch fire," he murmured into her ear.

Too late, Kari thought blissfully, and wondered if Brandon could feel her heart pounding next to his.

"I hope everything works out with our parents as well as it has for us," she said softly.

"We've done everything we could," Brandon said. "From now on, they're on their own. We have a more important relationship to worry about—ours."

And as they kissed again in the moonlight, Kari forgot about everything except the joy of discovering her very own romance.

We hope you enjoyed reading this book. If you would like to receive further information about available titles in the Bantam series, just write to the address below, with your name and address: Kim Prior, Bantam Books, 61–63 Uxbridge Road, Ealing, London W5 5SA.

If you live in Australia or New Zealand and would like more information about the series, please write to:

Sally Porter   Kiri Martin
Transworld Publishers   Transworld Publishers (NZ) Ltd
(Australia) Pty Ltd   3 William Pickering Drive
15–25 Helles Avenue   Albany
Moorebank   Auckland
NSW 2170   NEW ZEALAND
AUSTRALIA

All Bantam and Young Adult books are available at your bookshop or newsagent, or can be ordered from the following address: Corgi/Bantam Books, Cash Sales Department, PO Box 11, Falmouth, Cornwall, TR10 9EN.

Please list the title(s) you would like, and send together with a cheque or postal order to cover the cost of the book(s) plus postage and packing charges of £1.00 for one book, £1.50 for two books, and an additional 30p for each subsequent book ordered to a maximum of £3.00 for seven or more books.

(The above applies only to readers in the UK, and BFPO)

Overseas customers (including Eire), please allow £2.00 for postage and packing for the first book, an additional £1.00 for a second book, and 50p for each subsequent title ordered.